Capturing Magic

THE LEGACY OF ANDROVA

ALEX C. VICK

Dedication

For Imogen, I hope you always believe in magic

Contents

Prologue

Jax stepped through the portal from Androva into the half-light of a Terran summer's evening. Night would fall within the next hour, and the sky was already dark grey. He had not been able to wait any longer before coming to look for Shannon, despite the fact that it would have been safer in complete darkness. Where *was* she? If only they hadn't had that stupid argument.

Jax had opened the portal for Shannon that morning, but she hadn't turned up. And it was a really important day because they had been going to demonstrate their new Rejuvenation Spell in front of the Council. At first, Jax had blamed Shannon's absence on their argument the day before. He had been ready to apologise, but when Shannon failed to appear through the portal, he became angry with her. It wasn't until his anger had died down, much later that day, that he realised it was completely out of character for Shannon not to keep an appointment with the Council.

After that, he started to get worried. The more he thought about it, the more worried he got. But he couldn't go to look for her until it was dark enough that there would be no Terrans wandering about. And now here he was, and there was no sign of Shannon.

Then he noticed a letter propped against a nearby tree. Snatching it up in relief, he began to read. His relief soon turned to dismay.

"Dear Jax,

I imagine you are wondering what has happened to your friend Shannon? Well, she is with me. As my prisoner. I had hoped to be able to uncover the secret to becoming a magician from her, but it seems we are going to need your help. Don't tell anyone about this letter. If you disobey me, she will suffer. I might not be able to use magic yet, but I can still be <u>very</u> unpleasant. Be back where you found this letter at nightfall, and someone will collect you.

Regards,

Oh, you didn't really expect me to give my name, did you?"

1 The Seminary of Magic (Four Weeks Earlier)

"You have *got* to be kidding me," said Jax, looking scornfully at Professor Alver. "There is no way on Androva I'm doing that spell." He pushed his black hair impatiently off his forehead, then put his hands into his pockets, clenching them into fists.

Professor Alver looked back at Jax, his expression remaining calm, though there was a hint of amusement lifting one corner of his mouth. "And would you care to share with us all your reasons for refusing?" he asked, glancing behind Jax to the rest of the class.

There were ten other underage magicians seated on chairs around the training room. It was one of the smaller rooms in the Seminary of Magic, used mainly for teaching magic theory and some of the more contained and quieter spells.

The day was warm, and the sunlight shining through the high windows brightened the blue glow of the Protection Spell that enclosed the room.

Jax narrowed his green eyes briefly, struggling to keep his temper. He opened his mouth and then shut it again. "Yes?" prompted the professor, crossing one leg over the other as he settled back into his chair. He was dressed similarly to his students, in slim trousers and a shirt of dark cloth, his Sygnus glowing silvery-white near his shoulder. The professor's hair was a light brown, and his eyes sparkled with intelligence.

"It's ridiculous," Jax burst out, "it's stupid, it's *demeaning!*"

Some of the other magicians giggled, but they quickly stopped as the professor directed his steady gaze towards them. Then, raising his eyebrows, he turned back to Jax. "Indeed?" he asked evenly. "Please elaborate."

Jax stared for a moment at the square of bright pink material resting on the table next to the professor. It was not particularly large, but it was infused with enough magic to make the pink colour almost fluorescent. It was the most hideous shade that Jax had ever seen.

Androvan clothing tended to be on the conservative side to ensure visibility of the

Sygnus. The more Jax looked at the square of material, the more impossible the spell seemed. "I can't do it," he said flatly. "This is not the kind of magic I asked you to teach me. How is this going to help me to build an underground portal room on Terra? How is this going to help me do *anything*?"

His voice rose as he struggled to contain his frustration. The professor's expression became thoughtful as he waited for Jax to finish. "I see," he began. "Let me make sure I understand your objections. You say that you can't do it. Do you mean that the spell is too difficult for you?"

Jax glared at Professor Alver. "The spell is *not* too difficult for me," he answered, though as he spoke he knew that this was not entirely true. The spell was very advanced, and it would be a big challenge even for someone with as much natural magical ability as Jax possessed. There was no guarantee that Jax would be successful even if he agreed to try the spell.

Placing a Concealing Spell over his Sygnus, as Professor Alver had asked Jax to do, would not be straightforward. A Sygnus is not just a family symbol that represents a bloodline. It is also a magical key that can be used to unlock more sophisticated spells.

Traditionally each underage magician's first spell is to formally adopt their family Sygnus.

From then on it is magically engraved on every shirt or jacket they ever wear for the rest of their lives. It is meant to be visible at all times. It will resist any Concealing Spell with all its might.

The professor expected Jax to make the spell last for one entire day and night, which is an incredibly long time for a Concealing Spell. But Jax knew, and the professor knew, that the main problem was not the type of spell or its duration. The problem was the method of concealment. For a period of twenty-four hours Jax would have to cover his Sygnus with something so unbelievably pink, it would be visible to every single person within a hundred-metre radius.

"Alright," continued the professor, "let me address your next concern. You say that this is not the kind of magic you asked me to teach you. We agreed that I would teach you how to build a portal room underneath the Terran soil, did we not?"

Jax nodded. Professor Alver was one of the few magicians who possessed the ability to construct a portal room with magic. More importantly, he was the only one prepared to share that knowledge with Jax.

"And do you believe me capable of determining what spells need to be mastered along the way in order for you to achieve this?"

After a moment's hesitation, Jax nodded again.

Then he shook his head. "But I don't understand! Wearing that hideous thing will not teach me how to excavate an underground chamber!" Privately he thought that once his classmates had seen him walking around with that pink beacon on his shoulder, he would need to live underground for several weeks to get over the embarrassment. And how would he explain it to Shannon, his Terran girlfriend?

Some of the other underage magicians had started to snigger again at the thought of Jax wearing pink. Professor Alver raised his hand, and the noise stopped. "The Council has permitted significant changes at the Seminary in recent weeks. You have all felt the benefit of these changes. We are able to teach more advanced magic to underage magicians than has ever been allowed before."

The professor stood up and paused. "However…" he continued slowly. "However. You remain underage, and you still have a lot to learn." He inclined his head towards Jax and said, "One Spell of Removal does not a senior magician make." Then he smiled to take the edge off his words. "No matter how brave or life changing that spell may be."

Jax closed his eyes briefly. He remembered a small room at the foot of a cold, dark mountain, and the heart-stopping moment when he had desperately projected the Spell of Removal towards an ancient evil magician of unimaginable power. The twisted face of Angelus as he attempted to use his Death Spell on Shannon still haunted Jax in his nightmares.

"So," went on Professor Alver, "you will tackle the Concealing Spell. All of you. I will decide what you will each conceal, and for how long you will conceal it. Next time, if you prove yourselves suitably skilled, you may be lucky enough to follow Jax in his battle against vanity."

Jax frowned. "I'm not *vain*," he protested. "That's not the reason I don't want to use that pink monstrosity. It's because there's no purpose to it. I can do the spell without it!"

"I am sure that you can," responded Professor Alver. "But that is not the point. The point is whether you can do the spell *with* it. Can you master this difficult spell, when you don't actually *want* to succeed? Can you persuade your magic to follow the request of your teacher even though you think you will look ridiculous?"

He looked at Jax, making sure Jax understood. This was not just a question of magical skill, it was a question of discipline. Never a strong point for Jax, but unfortunately very necessary if a magician wanted to reach his or her full potential. Professor Alver had been more than a little like Jax in his younger years. He knew Jax did not yet understand the importance of self-control in channelling magical ability. The professor spoke again.

"Or perhaps you are not ready for this test. Perhaps I was wrong."

Jax clenched his fists tighter in his pockets. He glanced across at his best friend, Darius, who was trying not to laugh. Darius knew that Professor Alver was just the kind of teacher that Jax needed. And he was also looking forward to seeing Jax wearing pink. He had no doubt that his friend would succeed at the spell, difficult though it would be. But Jax could hardly blame him for finding the prospect of it all quite funny.

Darius wondered if he could manage to take a record of it with Shannon's mobile device. Jax and Darius were both intrigued with the Terran technology they had heard about so far, especially taking photos and videos. Unfortunately, Shannon's mobile seemed to stop working after going through the portal, and Jax and Darius were still trying to identify a suitable Protection Spell for it.

Jax gritted his teeth, but reluctantly admitted defeat. "OK, I'll do it," he replied to Professor Alver. "I may never live this down, but I'll do it all the same."

The professor smiled. "You have one week to master the spell," he told Jax. "Good luck."

The other underage magicians stepped forward to receive their individual assignments, with only Darius and one other, a girl called Cassia, being challenged to conceal their Sygnus symbols. The rest were given easier magical objects, and no one else was required to use such a flamboyant means of concealment as Jax.

Jax and Darius walked part of the way home together. It was a Friday afternoon at the beginning of summer, and classes were finished for the week. Jax continued to attract the occasional stare of recognition from other Androvans, even though it had been more than a month since he had battled Angelus alongside Shannon.

Androvans were gradually getting used to life without the threat of Angelus escaping constantly hanging over them. The Code of rules and regulations had been rewritten, and trips to Terra to harvest its magic were no longer needed. There was even talk of rebuilding the Foundation for Research. Jax really hoped that this would happen. He loved nothing more than experimenting with magic.

"Jax, Darius, wait up!" came a voice. Jax and Darius turned to see Hesta, another underage magician, running towards them. Her blonde hair fell around her shoulders as she came to a halt a few feet away. "Are you going straight home?"

she asked, looking disappointed.

"Well…" began Darius, "we kind of need to get started on our assignments. Shannon will be here tomorrow and we promised to help her prepare for her year one assessment."

Hesta's pale blue eyes flashed with annoyance, and she turned away for a second to hide her reaction. When she faced the boys again, she was smiling sweetly. "But I was really hoping you could show me your portal room spellstations. Professor Livia insists that I learn how to create my own. I was hoping that I could stay in her class with you, but apparently I've gone as far as I can in Combat," she finished, with a little pout.

Jax and Darius exchanged a look, both trying to keep a straight face. There were six disciplines in total at the Seminary of Magic. Every known spell was categorised within these six. On one side of the building were Remedies, Living Magic, and Combat. On the other side were Manipulation, History, and Physical. Each underage magician was required to attend classes in all six disciplines, but it was up to the professors to determine when each student had reached their full potential in a particular area.

Hesta was about as suited to Combat as a fish was suited to dry land. Her screams and hysterics when on the receiving end of anything more than the most basic of Containment Spells were well known. Jax and Darius found her amusing, but did not take her seriously as a magician.

Hesta, on the other hand, wanted Jax to be her boyfriend. He was the most promising underage magician at the Seminary, and when he turned his cool green-eyed stare in her direction, Hesta got butterflies in her stomach. Despite her limited magical ability, she was a very pretty girl with lots of friends. She couldn't understand his indifference, which had only increased since he had met Shannon. She was determined to get Jax to notice her, and didn't care what she had to do to make it happen.

"Look, Hesta," answered Jax apologetically, "I don't think we'll have time tonight. Alver's given me a nightmare Concealing Spell, and I still have to write my history assignment on portal creation. They won't let me build a portal room on Terra until I've proved that I understand all the implications."

Hesta shrugged, trying to look as if she didn't care. "Well, I suppose it can wait, but you have to promise me we can do it some other time." She turned to Darius, putting her hand on his arm. "It is Seminary protocol that we help another student when they ask, after all."

Darius blushed slightly as Hesta stared into his eyes. Then she turned to walk back the way she had come from, and the two boys continued home. Jax's thoughts immediately returned to Shannon, and he wondered what she was doing. She needed to pass the year one assessment to be able to join Jax and Darius in their classes, but she was finding the spells something of a challenge…

2 The Only Magician On Terra

Shannon looked exasperatedly at the giant toy bear in the corner of her bedroom. "You have *got* to be kidding me," she said, echoing the words that Jax had said at the Seminary the same afternoon. Her Augmentation Spell had got a little out of control.

The bear stared back at her, its large button eyes and rather stern mouth managing to convey an expression of indignation. It was now slightly taller than Shannon herself, and twice as wide.

Facing the bear's offended stare, Shannon was reminded of Mr. Charles, the headmaster at her school. "Shannon Blackwood, explain yourself," she imagined the bear saying.

"I didn't mean to make you this big. You were only supposed to double in size!" Shannon said helplessly. "This is a nightmare. What on earth am I supposed to do now?" Her hands were still giving off a silvery glow from the end of the spell, and she stared down at them. Then her head lifted back up sharply as she heard her mother's footsteps reaching the top of the stairs.

"Shannon?" called her mother. "Who are you talking to? I need to remind you about something."

Shannon turned back to the bear in a panic. Grabbing it around its rather large stomach, she tried to force it into her wardrobe. "Just a second!" she called, wrestling with the bear's arms and legs, which did not seem to want to fit behind the wardrobe door.

She was just pushing the wardrobe closed when her mother opened the bedroom door and put her head around it.

"Everything OK?" asked her mother with raised eyebrows.

Shannon, still leaning against the bulging wardrobe door, tried to adopt a casual pose.

"Um, yeah, everything's fine," she replied.

Her mother looked at Shannon suspiciously for a moment, and Shannon clenched her fists together in case any of her magic was still glowing in the palms of her hands.

"I thought I heard you talking to someone," Shannon's mother continued.

Shannon shrugged, looking blank, and her mother sighed with impatience. Shannon was only half listening. She was actually concentrating on pushing her magic force field right back inside her head, where there was no chance of her mother seeing it.

After the world-changing events of the previous month, the Androvan Council had suggested that Shannon complete her basic training at the Seminary before revealing her magical ability to anyone on Terra.

Shannon had wholeheartedly agreed with this suggestion. She was still coming to terms with everything herself and was quite happy to keep it a secret for now. However, this meant that she had to carry on as normal when she was on Terra, and that wasn't always easy.

"I wanted to remind you about the dinner tomorrow," said Shannon's mother, realising that she wasn't going to get a response from Shannon. "I don't know what your plans are for the day, but you *must* be back here by six o' clock at the latest."

Shannon frowned, then rolled her eyes as she remembered. "I don't see why *I* have to be here. It's not me going for the promotion, is it?"

"We've had this discussion," replied her mother, sighing again. "InterPharm is very hot on reinforcing its core values, and the division CEO wants to meet us all before confirming your father's new role. It's only one dinner, Shannon." Swallowing her irritation, she added, "I'm sure you can manage to do an impersonation of a well-behaved daughter for a few hours if you put your mind to it."

Shannon's behaviour over recent weeks had been deteriorating, and her parents were getting frustrated with it. As far as Shannon was concerned, all she wanted to do was practice spells, and the only place she wanted to be was on Androva.

The bright silver light generated by the magic inside her made everything on Terra seem dull and boring. It was proving kind of difficult to be the same quiet, well-behaved girl that she had been before. Constantly suppressing her magic so that it would remain undetected made her feel miserable.

And now she had this stupid dinner. On most Saturdays, including the evenings, she pretended to be with her best friend, Penny. But really she would be practicing magic with Jax and sometimes Darius. Now tomorrow evening she would be stuck at home making polite conversation with some dreary company executive.

"Fine, I'll be back home on time," she muttered ungraciously. Her mobile phone beeped with a text, and she reached over to the desk to pick it up, forgetting for a moment the bear in the wardrobe. The wardrobe door immediately sprang open, and Shannon gasped and leaned back to push it closed.

Fortunately her mother had already left to go back downstairs, her mind turning back to the dinner and what to cook.

The text was from Penny, who wanted to know what Shannon was doing for the weekend. Penny only knew half the story. Shannon had admitted to having a secret boyfriend that she didn't want her parents to know about yet, and Penny had willingly provided cover for Shannon. But she was desperate to meet Jax, and Shannon was running out of excuses.

It was only another two weeks until the school summer holidays started, and Shannon knew that Jax and Darius would expect to visit Terra properly. The two fourteen-year-old Androvan magicians couldn't wait to see Terra in daylight, but Shannon had mixed feelings about it.

On the one hand, she really wanted to show Terra off. Androva might be full of magicians and spells, but it had nothing to match Terra's superior technology and entertainment.

On the other hand, Jax and Darius stood little chance of blending in as ordinary teenagers. The way they looked and dressed was different, of course, but it was more than that.

Both boys, as accomplished magicians, radiated a faint energy from the internal force fields generated by their magic ability. You could only feel it if you got really close, but even from a distance it changed the air around them slightly. It was a bit like static electricity.

Shannon was used to it, but she knew that anyone paying attention would sense something different about them. They had been practicing suppressing their magic, like Shannon, but were not as good at it as she was.

Shannon replied to Penny's text, saying that she had to stay home on Saturday night for the dinner, but that maybe she would be free on Sunday. **"One of Dad's bosses coming to inspect our core values,"** she typed. **"Boring!!"**

"What are core values anyway???" replied Penny.

"Pretending to be perfect!?!" texted Shannon.

"Good luck with THAT!!!" said Penny's reply. Shannon grinned. She wondered what the InterPharm boss would think if he knew there was a secret underage magician in the family.

Shannon closed her bedroom door and turned back to the bear. She stared at it, hoping for inspiration. Her long hair, the same dark brown as her eyes, was tied back in a ponytail, revealing delicate silver earrings in her ears. They had been a present from Jax for her fourteenth birthday, and were made in the shape of his Sygnus. Their centres would spin, just like a real Sygnus, when Shannon carried out any advanced magic.

But the Augmentation Spell was not advanced magic. None of the year one assessment spells were advanced, and yet Shannon hadn't really mastered any of them. She was a powerful magician, and when a spell called for serious magic, Shannon had no problem.

Her Immobility Spell had already earned itself a place in Androvan history. Just ask a certain ex-Council member called Marcus. (On second thought, don't ask him, he's still pretty angry about it.)

It was the simple spells that she could not do. Shannon was well aware that a lot of Androvans would consider her a risk until she had proved that she could control the strength of her magic.

There were a few Council members who had started to raise concerns about Shannon, now that the initial excitement of Angelus's defeat had settled down. She was desperate to prove them wrong, but the giant bear staring at her so indignantly was not exactly going to change their minds.

Taking a deep breath, Shannon projected her magic as slowly and carefully as she could until her hands shone silver again. Cautiously, she filled the light with a Reduction Spell, and it turned very slightly darker. Some spells could change the colour of a magician's magic quite dramatically, but the basic spells did not.

Then she directed the spell slowly towards the bear, and in a split second, almost before Shannon realised what was happening, the bear had shrunk to the size of her thumb. "No, no, no!" she exclaimed, immediately closing her hands to cut off the spell before it touched anything else.

She picked up the now tiny bear and ground her teeth in frustration. This was not going well. Then suddenly she became aware that she was being watched. Turning her head, she saw her seven-year-old sister, Tammy, standing in the doorway with a look of astonishment on her face. Shannon closed her eyes for a moment. Could this evening get any worse?

"Shannon?" began Tammy eagerly, stepping forward. "What did you do to Boris the Bear?"

Shannon swallowed. "What do you think I did?" she asked, playing for time. She didn't know how long Tammy had been standing there.

"It looks like you put a spell on him to make him tiny!" responded Tammy, reaching out to touch the bear in Shannon's hands. "Did you? Can you do magic? Did you use fairy dust? Where did you learn it from? Can I do it too?" Her words were tumbling over themselves in her excitement.

Shannon started to panic. Desperately she tried to think of an excuse to explain what Tammy had seen. "It's not really magic," she started slowly, then sped up as she decided what to say.

"I was just practicing something for my next drama lesson at school. It's special effects, like when we go to the cinema and it seems like magic, but you know it's not really."

Tammy looked at her suspiciously. Then she lowered her head to examine the bear, and gave it a little shake. To Shannon's dismay, a faint mist of silver was released from the bear's fur. Tammy looked back at Shannon triumphantly.

"It's... it's just a trick," Shannon tried again. "I was only pretending..."

She trailed off, seeing from her sister's face that her excuses were not working. The problem, Shannon thought, was that Tammy actually believed in magic. If an adult had seen Shannon's Reduction Spell, they probably wouldn't have believed it and would readily accept an excuse to explain it away.

Tammy, however, took it for granted that magic and spells were perfectly possible. She was looking at Shannon with wide eyes, delighted at this unexpected turn of events.

Shannon closed her bedroom door again and sat down on the bed. Taking Tammy's hand, she pulled her sister down to sit alongside her. "Look," she began, "this is the biggest secret you will ever know. You have to double, triple promise me that you will never tell anyone. Do you understand?"

Tammy nodded with a serious expression. Shannon sighed. Tammy was absolutely terrible at keeping secrets. It was like they wriggled around inside her head until she felt as if she would go crazy unless she told someone. Shannon knew this, but she had to try.

It was far too soon for anyone to know about Androva, and Shannon being a magician. Or about the fact that she had recently nearly died saving the entire world from an evil maniac.

"The thing is, Tammy," she continued. "What you saw might have looked like magic—"

"It *was* magic!" Tammy interrupted.

"OK, so *maybe* it was magic," Shannon admitted. Tammy's face lit up. "But you can't tell anyone about it, you can't think about it, you can't even dream about it," Shannon said urgently. "You have to trust me, because it's just not the right time for anyone to know."

"But I want to do it too!" Tammy cried. "Please, Shannon, please teach me how to do it!"

Shannon groaned inwardly. "The thing is," she said evenly, trying to calm Tammy down, "I'm still learning all about it myself. I won't be ready to teach anyone else for a while. It could be dangerous. I mean, incredibly dangerous." Tammy looked uncertain. Shannon paused, wondering how she could really put Tammy off. "Like, what if I shrunk Jenny the Elephant down to the same size as Boris the Bear? She might get sucked up in the vacuum cleaner," she added dramatically. Jenny was Tammy's favourite bedtime toy.

Tammy backed away from Shannon, looking as if she might cry. Shannon suddenly went cold, realising that until she got her magic under control, a horrible accident might actually happen. She didn't even know for sure if the Reduction Spell worked on people as well as objects. She took a shaky breath, pushing the force field even further down inside her head, which then started to hurt.

"Come on," she said, standing up. "Dinner's probably ready by now. We can talk about it later." Tammy looked at Shannon for a moment, her lip wobbling. Then she brightened, remembering that tonight's dinner was spaghetti bolognese, one of her favourites. Shannon gave her a hug and, holding her breath, hoped that Tammy would allow herself to be distracted.

Her sister was usually a bit like a butterfly, flitting from one topic to another, so there was a good chance that Shannon could successfully change the subject. She sighed with relief when Tammy skipped out of the room, talking about a birthday party that she was going to the following afternoon.

Shannon followed her down the stairs, her legs trembling a bit. She decided not to do any more spells until she went to Androva the following morning. Perhaps Jax and Darius would have figured out how she could weaken her magic to make the simple spells less dangerous. She could only hope Tammy would keep it all secret for a little while at least.

3 Finding The Right Spell

Saturday morning dawned bright and sunny. The first thing Jax saw when he opened his eyes was the square of pink material for his Concealing Spell draped over the windowsill to the right of his bed.

The windows themselves were impressively large, extending from knee height all the way to the top of the high ceiling, and the view to Sandro's Mountain in the distance was breathtaking.

Jax paid no attention to the view, however. All he could see was the pink material glittering malevolently in the morning sunshine.

Jax had failed completely to carry out the Concealing Spell the previous evening, and he felt as if the bright pink colour was now mocking him. If he couldn't do the spell inside Mabre House, where no one could see him, what chance did he have of achieving it outside in the city, or at the Seminary?

He sighed with frustration, then slowly extended one arm, turning his palm upwards to project a simple Manipulation Spell. The curtain, obeying his spell, moved across until the pink was covered.

Then he rolled onto his back and looked up at the multicoloured ceiling, gathering his thoughts for the day ahead. The swirling mists of various unfinished spells usually had a calming effect, but today his impatience persisted.

He was so fed up with *waiting*. He wanted to build that portal room on Terra today. He wanted Shannon to be free to come to Androva whenever she wanted. He wanted to be free to go to Terra whenever he wanted. Everything was happening so slowly.

Eventually he got up, realising that there was no point in allowing his frustration to turn to anger. Saturday was one of the few days that he and Shannon could usually spend together, and he knew she would not appreciate it if he was in a bad mood when she arrived. Anyway, he had to go and open the portal to Terra in an hour or so, which meant he might as well get dressed and have some breakfast.

Androvan food was very simple, with breakfast usually consisting of bread, cheese, and fruit. There was no need for Androvans to create endless choices or sophisticated meals when they could always use spells to experiment with taste, colour, and texture.

The Council did not permit food and drink to be filled with Manipulation Spells, except for the approved list of remedies. Still, underage magicians had a lot of fun at the Seminary inventing extraordinary (but harmless) feasts and banquets for their professors and each other.

Shannon sometimes brought Terran snack food for Jax and Darius to try, which had so far had mixed results. Both boys had been horrified at their first taste of liquorice, but chocolate, on the other hand, had been an overwhelming success. Because the cacao tree did not grow on Androva, Darius had been unsuccessfully trying to recreate the taste of chocolate with magic ever since.

After his breakfast, Jax descended the stairs to the underground portal room. He was feeling much better, and looking forward to seeing Shannon. They had an agreement regarding portal opening times, which both had promised the Council they would not deviate from. The risk that an unsuspecting

Terran could walk into the open portal was too great for it to be left open all the time.

Unfortunately this meant that if Shannon missed the window when the portal was open, she was stuck on Terra, with no way to get a message to Jax until the next agreed opening time.

On several occasions she had completely lost her temper with her parents for changing their arrangements and preventing her from going to Androva. This was part of the reason why they were finding Shannon's behaviour so challenging recently.

Jax checked the time and carried out the opening sequence, lighting up each of the magical symbols in turn. As soon as the spellstation had created the doorway, which shimmered in front of him, Shannon fell through it, and he stumbled backwards for a moment, holding onto her.

Shannon ducked her head in embarrassment, her hair falling forward as she steadied herself. She was always a bit shy when she first saw Jax after a few days apart.

"Hey." He grinned, gently lifting her chin upwards so he could look into her eyes. "I know I'm spectacular and all that, but couldn't you play a *little* hard to get?"

Shannon immediately put up her hands

and pushed herself backwards. "You do realise," she retorted crossly, her shyness forgotten, "I only had to grab onto you because you were late opening the portal. You try balancing between two worlds and see if you can stay upright, *Mr. Spectacular*," she finished sarcastically.

Jax laughed, and then so did Shannon. He leaned towards her for a kiss. Shannon's heart was racing when Jax lifted his head up again. For a moment all her fears about the year one assessment and Tammy were totally forgotten.

Jax's smile was dazzling in the dim light of the portal room. "I suppose we'd better go to the training room," he said finally. "Although it does seem stupid to be stuck indoors when the sun is shining."

"Maybe we could eat lunch outside?" suggested Shannon as they started to climb the winding staircase.

"Did you bring some crazy new Terran food for me to try?" asked Jax, turning back to face her.

Shannon patted the back pocket of her jeans, which rustled. "Jelly Babies," she responded. Jax raised his eyebrows. "What?" he replied incredulously. "Babies made out of jelly? Actually, don't answer that. I'm not sure

I even want to know."

Shannon giggled. Sometimes she deliberately chose weird English snacks for Jax and Darius to try, just to see the look on their faces. There were so many differences between their two worlds.

Shannon had now been to Androva several times. But the only people she really spent time with were Jax and Darius, and Professor Lenora, who had been assigned by the Council to tutor Shannon for her year one assessment.

She had met with the Council twice to review her progress, but she had not spent time with any other underage magicians yet. It was hoped that she could start to attend the Seminary properly after passing her assessment.

The Council were trying not to monitor Shannon and Jax too closely. Everyone was grateful that the dark years spent living under the threat of Angelus were over. But some Council members, and in particular Revus, Jax's father, wanted to be cautious. It wasn't expressly forbidden for Shannon to start using magic on Terra, but it definitely wasn't being encouraged either.

She would have had a lot more freedom to come to Androva if she had been able to use Distraction Spells, which would prevent anyone from even noticing her absence. She had used one before, on a custodian on Androva, so she understood in principle how they worked.

Though they were on the list of Unauthorised Spells, exceptions could be made if the Council agreed. But she was nervous of upsetting the Council, and she was also becoming uneasy about the strength of her magic. It had grown significantly, and she knew that was partly her own fault.

To prepare for the confrontation with Angelus, Shannon had harvested some living green magic and joined it to her own. Such a thing had never been done before. She had already been showing signs of being a formidable magician, but now her power was at a level that was almost unheard of.

Living magic exists in every tree and plant, and the taller and greener the tree, the greater the magic it possesses. Androva does not have many trees, therefore its supplies of living magic are low.

Terra, of course, has an endless supply. However, as there are still no magicians on Terra except for Shannon, it remains a long-kept secret.

Until recently, Androvans would visit

Terra at night to harvest its living magic. The harvested magic was used to contain Angelus, according to a centuries-old treaty between the two worlds.

All this meant that things were difficult for Shannon. She felt as if she were half living her life as a magician and half living her old, normal life, without being able to really enjoy either one.

She frowned with concentration, determined to somehow figure out a way to control her magic ability. Jax, noticing the frown, took her hand.

"We'll fix this," he said firmly, knowing exactly what she was thinking about. "I know you're worried, but between us we'll discover the answer."

They entered the training room. It was the size of a large hall, with high ceilings and windows. Jax walked to the middle of the room, then turned back to face Shannon.

"So," he began. "The year one assessment covers all six disciplines." He held up his fingers and counted as he listed them. "Remedies, Living Magic, and Combat, plus Manipulation, History, and Physical.

"We know there won't be a problem with Combat," he said with a grin. Shannon shrugged her shoulders, but couldn't help smiling back. There were three main Combat Spells: Containment, Scattering, and Immobility. Shannon could use and escape from all three, and had previously done so to quite dramatic effect.

"Physical for year one is the entry-level Solo Transference spell," continued Jax, "which was the first thing I taught you." Shannon remembered it for a moment. Floating up to the ceiling, propelled by the dazzling silver glow of her brand new magical force field. That was the moment she had started to really believe in magic.

"History isn't exactly difficult," Jax said next. "You've read enough books from the Repository of Records by now to pass the assessment easily."

Jax and Shannon regularly swapped books, with Jax getting by far the better deal. He lent Shannon the Androvan history books she needed to read for her assessment, and she provided him with a variety of fiction books in return. Until recently, fiction and storybooks had been forbidden on Androva, and Jax was very much enjoying the imaginary worlds created by Shannon's favourite Terran authors.

"Living Magic is the basic Harvesting Spell, and you can obviously do that," Jax went on. "Manipulation is where we're stuck.

"The basic spells are Augmentation, Reduction, Cleaning, and Repairing. They're not going to let you even try to create any remedies, until you've proved you have enough control for the Manipulation Spells."

Shannon nodded. "I tried Augmentation and Reduction again last night, but it was hopeless." She paused, wondering whether she should tell Jax about Tammy. But Jax had already started speaking again.

"I wonder if there is a way to make it harder for you, to somehow reduce your power, and then your spell would be weaker? I don't know how to make the spells more difficult though. They're just so basic," he continued exasperatedly. "Unless…"

"What?" prompted Shannon. "What are you thinking?"

"It might work," replied Jax, looking more animated as the idea took shape in his mind. "It just might!"

He walked closer to Shannon and started to explain. "I think part of the problem is that you've only ever known your magic to be powerful. You went so quickly from the initial spark. Within one week you were keeping up with me and Darius."

Shannon agreed. "I remember that your

father said it was very fast," she added.

"You never experienced those first months when it's supposed to be weaker. When you can practice all day long and never do any real harm. I think that's why you're struggling to moderate your magic now, because you don't have that experience."

"OK, so how do I learn then?" asked Shannon.

"Let me project a Scattering Spell on you. Let me break up your magic so you can only use a small part of it. Then, with some practice, you might be able to learn how to do it on your own," he suggested.

Shannon thought for a moment. Then she nodded. She had nothing to lose after all. They were in a training room, and the blue Protection Spell would prevent any permanent harm.

The Scattering Spell, like all three of the Combat spells, is designed to incapacitate another magician's ability. It splits your opponent's magic into fragments, and they have to really focus their mind to draw it all back together.

Jax stepped back several paces towards the middle of the room. He concentrated for a few seconds, and his hands started to glow. Shannon felt her muscles grow tense with anticipation. "Don't defend yourself," warned Jax. "You have to let the spell work." Shannon tried to relax.

Then, without warning, Jax sent the spell hurtling in Shannon's direction. Instinctively she resisted it, despite herself, clenching her fists and drawing the force field back together.

Then she sent a Containment Spell straight back to Jax in return. A bright white band of magic tightened ruthlessly inside his head, and he staggered back with an angry yell.

"I said *don't* defend yourself!" he shouted.

Shannon blushed and immediately dropped her spell. She and Jax looked at each other, before Jax reluctantly started to laugh. "That went well," he said sarcastically.

Shannon apologised. "I'm really sorry. I don't know why I did that," she said. "I couldn't help it. Please can we try again?"

4 A Seed Of Doubt

Jax raised his hands, and they started to glow again. This time it was better. Shannon remained still as Jax's Scattering Spell took effect. It was hard not to panic, feeling her magic dispersing like dust, but she managed it. Then, as Jax held the spell in place, she tried an Augmentation Spell on a book that was lying on the floor at the edge of the room.

At first, nothing happened. After a few minutes, with no change in the size of the book, Shannon stamped her foot in frustration. Jax tried not to smile, knowing that he couldn't get distracted if he was going to maintain his Scattering Spell.

The training room was quiet as the two underage magicians concentrated. The minutes passed. Then, eventually, just as Jax was about to suggest they take a break, Shannon got it. All of a sudden she could read the difference in her magic, and then she realised she could manipulate it as well.

Growing in confidence, she increased the size of the book bit by bit, then gradually reduced it again. Triumphantly she turned to Jax, her face shining. He dropped his spell and grinned back at her.

"Again," he urged, pointing to the window nearest to them, high up on the wall. It had a small crack in the glass. "Repairing Spell," he ordered, "straight away, before you forget how to do it."

Shannon took a breath and lifted her hands. She felt the magic energy buzzing inside her head, travelling down her arms to her hands. Tipping her head to one side slightly, she closed her eyes, trying to recreate the effects of the Scattering Spell.

When she was sure it was working, she opened her eyes again and projected the Repairing Spell at the window. It hovered for a moment before doing its job absolutely perfectly.

Jax made Shannon carry on with several more practice spells before he allowed her to stop.

"Not bad," he said cheerfully, adding, "for a Terran, of course." Shannon scowled, raising her hands as if to project another Containment Spell. Jax backed away, pretending to be scared, and Shannon grinned. Then she sighed with relief and dropped down to sit on the floor. Resting her chin in her hands, she looked across at Jax, who came to sit next to her.

"For a moment there, I thought I would never get it," she admitted.

"For a moment there, so did I," replied Jax. "I've never held a Combat Spell for so long before." Then his face took on a determined expression.

Shannon half groaned. "I know that look," she said. "What is it now? I'm kind of exhausted here."

"One final test," Jax suggested. "Cleaning Spell. On me."

Shannon immediately shook her head. "No way," she replied.

Androvans used the Cleaning Spell on themselves all the time. There was no need to take a shower or clean your teeth, wash your clothes, or even brush your hair, when a spell could do it all for you. It was a massive time saver.

Shannon had actually been looking forward to using it on herself, especially if it meant she could set her alarm clock fifteen minutes later in the morning. But the prospect of trying her first personal Cleaning Spell on Jax was a bit daunting.

"No," she repeated. "I'd rather try it on myself than try it on you. What if it goes wrong?"

Jax shrugged. "We're in a training room anyway—the damage won't be permanent. If you can do this last spell, you'll be ready for the assessment."

"Really?" asked Shannon suspiciously. "If it goes wrong, and your hair and clothes go completely crazy, are you actually telling me you won't mind?"

Jax smirked. "Well, maybe I might mind a little bit. But it's not as if anyone important will see me, is it?"

Shannon bristled. "Am I not important then?" she said, crossing her arms.

Jax rolled his eyes. "That's not what I meant and you know it," he replied.

Shannon stood up. "Alright," she said firmly. "Get up, and let's do this."

Jax got to his feet and waited expectantly. Shannon carefully projected the spell. It encircled Jax like a spinning cloud of silver. It was working fine, and she relaxed slightly, waiting for the spell to finish. Then she had an idea, and her mouth curved in a mischievous smile.

Carefully she increased the power of the spell. Jax was standing calmly, glad that it was going so well. At first he didn't notice anything, but he gradually became aware that the spell's gentle pressure was getting stronger. Eventually it was too noticeable to ignore.

"Shannon…" he warned, "what are you doing?"

Shannon took a couple of steps backwards and finished the spell with one final surge of strength that nearly knocked Jax off his feet. When the glow cleared, she burst out laughing.

Jax's hair was standing on end as if he had received an electric shock, and his clothes were wrapped around him like bandages. The expression of outrage on his face only made Shannon laugh more.

"I'm sorry!" she gasped, clutching her sides. "It was just too good an opportunity to resist!"

"You've asked for it now," threatened Jax, walking towards her. "You'll have purple hair and green skin by the time I've finished with you!"

Shannon screamed and ran away from him, still laughing. He caught up with her and they fell to the floor, Shannon trying to escape the spell that Jax was projecting.

Suddenly someone coughed in the doorway. Jax and Shannon turned to look and saw Revus standing there with a disapproving look on his face. His black hair, threaded with grey, was brushed straight back from his forehead, and he stood very upright. They scrambled to their feet, Jax doing his best to smooth down his hair. For a moment there was silence.

Revus was trying hard to rebuild his

relationship with his son, which had been pretty bad before the battle against Angelus a month ago. Jax's mother had died when he was very young, and Revus had been a rather strict, uncompromising father.

Jax, being Jax, had rebelled against Revus and all his rules, which had not made for a happy father-son relationship. Revus was now attempting to be less strict with Jax, but it did not come naturally to him.

"Yes, Father?" said Jax, breaking the silence.

Revus cleared his throat. "I just wanted to let you know that Professor Lenora is now free this afternoon to give Shannon an extra lesson. I'm sorry to have interrupted you," he said awkwardly, and turned to leave.

Jax and Shannon waited until he had gone, then started laughing. "It's like he sucks all the joy out of the room," said Jax exasperatedly. "I know he's trying, but honestly it's as if I'm living with a statue sometimes. He hardly ever smiles."

Although Shannon had laughed, she felt a bit bad for Revus. She knew better than anyone that Jax had his faults too, and he didn't always make it easy for his father.

"Can we have something to eat?" asked Shannon. "It must be lunchtime by now. Anyway, I need a break if I'm going to have to go to the Seminary this afternoon."

Jax agreed, and they made their way to the kitchen. After eating, they went outside, having decided to walk to the Seminary rather than use the portal room. It wasn't too far, and the sun was still shining.

Shannon always enjoyed the chance to see a bit more of Androva's capital city, and as long as she was with Jax, she didn't mind the curious looks she attracted.

Most people now knew all about what had happened, or at least they knew the less controversial report that the Council had since circulated. And it was obvious that Shannon wasn't from Androva, because she had no Sygnus.

She usually wore jeans, and a brightly coloured T-shirt, sometimes with a logo or other writing on it. This was quite different from the clothing worn on Androva.

After some deliberation, Jax had consented to try a Jelly Baby. He declared it was like eating a rubbery, sugary bug, and refused to have a second one. Shannon finished the packet herself, laughing at his shocked expression as she proceeded to bite all the heads off first.

"Can we drop in on Darius?" she asked as they set off. Jax nodded. "Of course," he replied. "I wanted to ask him round tonight anyway. I was hoping you could both help me figure out this

Concealing Spell that Alver set me yesterday."

Shannon was about to agree, when she remembered the dinner. "I can't," she said, annoyed. "I have to be back home for this stupid dinner with my dad's new boss."

"What?" asked Jax. "You have to meet your father's employer? Is that usual on Terra?"

"Not really," answered Shannon. "I mean, it's not unheard of, but having to go to a dinner is a bit over the top. It's just that he's getting promoted and his company have this thing about only promoting the right people.

"I have to be polite, well-behaved, and not say anything that contradicts the company's core values," she finished, repeating her mother's instructions in a sarcastic voice.

Jax snorted with laughter. "You?" he said. "Polite?"

Shannon gave him an indignant nudge with her elbow. "I can be polite," she retorted.

"Not these days. Maybe if you were under the influence of a Manipulation Spell," Jax said, still laughing.

"Well, I have to go back anyway," Shannon replied grumpily.

Jax asked her to explain exactly what her father did for a living. It was not a subject they had really talked about before, and Shannon tried to describe the InterPharm business.

It was a global pharmaceutical company, that made all kinds of drugs and medicines. Anything from lifesaving hospital therapies to cosmetic treatments. Shannon's father worked in Business Development, which meant researching and selling new products.

"So it's kind of like Remedies without the magic part," Jax suggested.

Shannon nodded. "I guess so."

"And what are these famous core values?" asked Jax.

"Honesty, Respect, and Teamwork," Shannon repeated. She knew them off by heart, thanks to regular reminders from her parents.

"My father would love those," replied Jax. "Though I hope you're not planning to stick to the Honesty part. Spells at the dinner table would definitely ruin your father's chances!"

They carried on walking until they reached the house where Darius lived. The city was laid out to a very open plan, and the buildings were not too close together.

Most were three stories tall or less, even at the centre, where the Council offices and the Seminary were located. Though the designs were different, each was built out of stone with a sloping slate roof, in all different shades from palest white to the darkest black.

Jax and Shannon went round to a side door.

He and Darius had been friends since they were very young, and they each knew the other's house as well as their own. Jax called for Darius as they entered the hallway, and his friend soon appeared at the top of the stairs.

Darius was the complete opposite of Jax in appearance and temperament. He had blond hair and calm dark blue eyes, plus a respect for authority that Jax had never quite managed to acquire. He grinned when he saw the two of them, and was about to say hello, when a girl appeared behind him, touching his shoulder.

It was Hesta. She gave Jax and Shannon a dazzling smile, saying excitedly, "Oh wow, you must be Shannon! I've heard so much about you. It's so great to finally meet you!"

Shannon looked at Jax, feeling a bit taken aback by the enthusiasm of Hesta's welcome. Jax was frowning slightly. "Hesta," he acknowledged. "I didn't know you would be here."

"She came round to see if I had time to show her my spellstation," explained Darius. "Remember, she asked us yesterday?"

He turned to smile at Hesta. "It's gone really well, hasn't it? I think you're making real progress. You'll soon be able to get your own spellstation working."

Hesta smiled back at him, saying, "Darius has been brilliant. I couldn't have asked for a better teacher." She squeezed his hand, and he looked a bit embarrassed, but pleased nonetheless.

Then Hesta ran lightly down the stairs to reach Jax and Shannon. Taking Shannon's hand, she pulled her down the hallway to the kitchen.

"Let's get something to drink," she said, "and then you can tell me all about yourself. I've got a feeling we're going to be good friends."

Turning back to Jax, she said, "Don't worry, I'll look after her. You can go and talk to Darius for a while." Jax caught Shannon's eye and gave a small shrug. He thought he might as well give Shannon the chance to get to know Hesta a little bit.

They were all the same age, and Hesta was very popular. If she befriended Shannon, it would help Shannon when she eventually attended the Seminary.

As Jax climbed the stairs towards Darius, his mind already turning back to the challenging Concealing Spell he had to master, Hesta and Shannon entered the kitchen.

It was a warm, welcoming room with a yellow stone floor. Dishes, plates, and cups were neatly stacked on a wooden table in the centre, obviously the result of a Cleaning Spell used after the lunchtime meal. Letting go of Shannon's arm, Hesta turned. Her pretty features became hard, and her eyes narrowed.

"Just so we're clear," she said in a low voice, "I've known Jax for a lot longer than you, and he is going to get bored of you very soon."

Putting her hands on her hips, she continued. "You're a joke anyway, thinking you can come to Androva and be a real magician. Don't you know what people are saying about you? If you had any self-respect, you'd accept the Spell of Removal and go back to being a nobody on Terra."

Shannon moved backwards, taking another step further away from Hesta with each horrible sentence that she uttered. It was as if Hesta had looked into her mind and was repeating each of her worst fears back to her. Her eyes began to fill with tears.

Hesta looked at her pityingly. "You know I'm right, don't you?" she said.

5 Professor Lenora

Shannon fought the urge to turn and run away from the terrible things Hesta was saying. She had been completely taken by surprise at the suddenness of Hesta's attack.

It felt like she was eleven years old again, in her first term at secondary school, being bullied by a group of year ten girls who had decided that she looked like a geek. The attack back then had come out of nowhere too. But this time the stakes were much higher.

At school, Shannon had endured the bullying for only two weeks before her best friend, Penny, had realised what was happening and joined forces with Shannon to fight the bullies off. But she still remembered those two weeks in horrible detail.

The bullies had told her that no one would want to be friends with someone who looked like her. They'd sneered at Shannon to go home and never come back, following her down the corridors every time they found her on her own. Shannon hadn't talked to Penny or any of her other friends about it because she had been too scared that the bullies were right.

Night after night she'd tried to change her hair and uniform, so that she wouldn't look like the geek she was accused of being. Then she would cry herself to sleep afterwards.

Hesta folded her arms and stared at Shannon. Then she glanced pointedly down at her Sygnus, which was in the shape of an elegant diamond, with curling lines at its centre. It was as if she wanted to draw Shannon's attention to it, to emphasise that Shannon didn't have one.

"Are you crying, Terran?" she asked mockingly.

Shannon flinched. When Jax called her "Terran," it was always said affectionately, but Hesta made it sound like the worst kind of insult. Shannon looked at the floor, trying to decide what to do.

If she allowed Hesta to bully her now, she might as well give up on the whole idea of being a magician and being part of Jax's life. Yes, she was afraid. But that didn't mean she was a coward.

Shannon lifted her head and looked Hesta in the eyes. "If you know so much about me, then

I'm surprised you have the guts to speak to me like that," she said evenly. Part of her wanted to crush Hesta with a brutal Containment Spell, but she knew that wouldn't help matters in the long run.

"I'm only telling you the truth," replied Hesta, tossing her head arrogantly. "Jax has a different girlfriend every time the season changes, and I've heard his own father wishes he could send you back to Terra and close the portal forever."

Shannon swallowed. "Why are you doing this?" she asked. Hesta didn't answer. Shannon saw a flicker of something on Hesta's face that she couldn't identify at first. Then all at once she realised what it was.

Hesta was jealous. She wanted Jax for herself! Well, thought Shannon, it doesn't make Hesta any less dangerous, but at least I know why she's attacking me like this. The two girls were silent for a moment.

Suddenly Jax and Darius could be heard coming down the stairs. "Shannon?" said Jax as he entered the kitchen. "We need to leave if we're going to make it to the Seminary..." He trailed off, realising that something was wrong.

Hesta recovered almost immediately. Shannon watched her expression change back to one of such genuine-looking friendliness that she nearly laughed in disbelief.

"Jax, we were just going to call you," Hesta began. "I thought Darius and I could walk with you, it's such a beautiful day. Then I could get to know Shannon a bit better. What do you think?"

Jax turned to Shannon enquiringly, looking pleased. "Is that OK with you?" he asked. Shannon didn't know what to say. Hesta was smiling so sweetly at her, and Jax obviously wanted the two of them to be friends.

If Shannon tried to tell Jax how nasty Hesta had just been, she thought there was a pretty good chance Jax wouldn't believe her.

"Um, OK," she managed. To her annoyance she saw a gleam of triumph in Hesta's eyes as the four of them left the house together.

Fortunately the walk to the Seminary was quite short, and Hesta easily kept the conversation going with a stream of inconsequential chatter. She made Jax laugh a couple of times, and Shannon said less and less, her heart sinking.

Eventually Jax put his arm round Shannon and asked her if she was OK. She put her head on his shoulder as they walked, feeling a bit better.

When the Seminary came into view, Shannon forgot her worries for a moment. She had been awestruck when she first saw the building, and that hadn't changed on subsequent visits. It was built entirely of black stone, in the shape of a large H, and it shimmered a little in the sunshine.

Three out of the six disciplines were arranged down either side of the H. Across the middle there were rooms for the professors and for underage magicians to eat and study in. The entranceway was a large arch, with Seminary of Magic carved in swirling silver letters across the top.

The admission ritual was quite straightforward, but Shannon had found it really exciting. When she'd first realised she was actually going to a school that taught magic, she could hardly breathe for nerves and anticipation.

Each underage magician had to write their name in front of them, in magic, and hold the silver letters in the air for at least one minute. If you could manage that, then your magic was strong enough to start the year one lessons.

Jax liked to boast that he was the youngest underage magician on record to be admitted to the Seminary. Darius never failed to point out that having a three-letter name was a completely unfair advantage!

Walking through the archway and into the silent Seminary building, Shannon took a deep breath. The air was always faintly charged with the residue of a hundred spells, and it never failed to put a smile on her face. Even Hesta couldn't change that.

As they started to walk to Professor Lenora's

room, Hesta interrupted, saying that she needed to get back home.

"It's been so wonderful to finally meet you though," she said to Shannon. "I can see why Jax and Darius think so highly of you."

Shannon had no idea how to respond to such blatant dishonesty. She looked at Jax for a second, disappointed that he didn't realise Hesta was lying. She mumbled something about being pleased to have met Hesta too, and watched the other girl walk confidently away, her blonde hair swishing from side to side.

"I'm really glad you met Hesta," said Jax, squeezing Shannon's arm. "She knows everyone, and it will make things much easier when you join the Seminary properly."

"That's true," agreed Darius. "I couldn't believe it when she turned up today. I told her you might come by, but she said she would probably have to leave before you got there. So isn't it lucky that you got to meet her after all?"

"Yeah," muttered Shannon, scuffing the floor with her foot. "Really lucky."

"Hey," protested Jax. "What's the problem?"

Shannon opened her mouth to tell him what had happened between her and Hesta earlier, but before she could start, Jax began speaking again.

"Look, I know she's a bit of an airhead, and her magic ability is pretty laughable. But just because I don't rate her, it doesn't mean that you can't be friends."

A slow smile spread across Shannon's face as she listened to Jax. "You don't rate her?" she repeated. "She's not a powerful magician either?"

Jax shook his head. "But you can't let my opinion stop you from making new friends here," he continued seriously. "Like I said, she knows everyone."

Shannon laughed with relief. Suddenly it didn't seem so important to tell Jax about what Hesta had said to her. The best revenge would be to ignore her. She had a feeling that being ignored was one of the things Hesta hated most.

"What's so funny?" asked Jax.

"I'll tell you later," said Shannon, smiling even more widely. "Come on, we're going to be late! Last one there has to eat a stick of liquorice!"

She turned and ran down the corridor. Jax and Darius glanced at each other, puzzled, but then ran after her, catching Shannon's sudden good mood.

All three were out of breath and laughing when they reached the Professor's room, Darius refusing to accept that he was the one who had to eat the liquorice.

Professor Lenora opened her door on hearing the noise, smiling tolerantly as she waited for the three underage magicians to notice her. She was one of the younger professors at the Seminary, like Professor Alver, and had a slim build, with her red hair pulled severely back.

She shared Alver's view that Shannon deserved the chance to prove that she could follow Seminary rules and abide by the Code.

The Council had agreed to Lenora being Shannon's tutor, as Lenora was one of the rare magicians who was good at the Spell of Immobility. It was thought that she might have a chance of being able to contain Shannon's magic if it ever got out of control.

The professor was still optimistic, however, that Shannon would be able to learn how to control her own magic, and had so far taken a very gentle approach to the lessons.

Shannon noticed the professor watching them, and she hastily nudged Jax and Darius. The boys usually stayed with her during her lessons, both for moral support and so that they could help her practice afterwards.

"Shannon," said Professor Lenora warmly. "You got the message then?"

Shannon nodded. The professor beckoned them in and closed the door behind them. Sunshine spilled through the large window, warming the plants lining the shelves on the opposite side of the room.

The small brightly coloured flowers looked like

jewels against the black stone of the walls, and did not resemble anything Shannon had seen on her own world. Professor Lenora specialised in Living Magic and was always researching how to strengthen Androva's supply of it.

Sitting down, she folded her hands in her lap. "How have you been getting on?" she asked. "Have you made any progress with the Manipulation Spells?"

Shannon glanced at Jax, then turned back to the professor excitedly. "Yes!" she responded, her facing lighting up. "Jax had this great idea how I could experience what a year one magician usually feels like when their magic is brand new. And it totally worked."

She turned to look at Jax again, who tried to look modest, but didn't really succeed. Darius rolled his eyes. The last thing Jax needed was for his ego to get any bigger. Then he remembered the Concealing Spell that Jax still had to do, and he felt a bit better.

"This is very good news, Shannon," said the professor, leaning forward. "Very good. How confident are you that you can succeed? I have to give the Council an update on Monday, and if you could pass the assessment this very afternoon it would go a long way to calming their fears."

"Well, I obviously haven't done Remedies

yet…" began Shannon hesitantly.

The professor waved her hand dismissively, saying, "If you can pass the other five disciplines, I will set you a Remedies assignment to take home with you. The Remedies discipline is not the main concern of the Council."

She stood up and waited expectantly. "Shall we go to the training room?"

6 The Dinner

Shannon swallowed nervously. There was no real reason to delay. At least she would be able to get it over with. They followed the professor back down the corridor to one of the larger training rooms that was also used for assessments. The high ceiling was necessary to test Solo Transference.

Professor Lenora wasted no time in getting started. Almost before Shannon realised it, she had flown past Physical, History, and Combat. The professor rubbed her temples after Shannon's Containment Spell, which, in her nervousness, Shannon had made far too powerful.

"I'm sorry," Shannon said anxiously, but the professor shook her head.

"It's fine," she replied, hiding her shock at the strength of magic that Shannon possessed.

Then it was on to Living Magic. Professor

Lenora had brought one of her plants into the training room, and Shannon reached out to it carefully.

The leaves began to give off a gentle glow, which tingled against her palms as she drew out the living magic inside them. The professor stopped Shannon before she went any further so that the magic energy could return back to the plant.

Finally, it was time for Manipulation. Five china cups of different sizes were placed on a low table in front of Shannon. The cups were white, with a twisting black pattern around the rim. The smallest was the size of a bottle cap, and the largest was the size of a bucket.

Shannon was asked to match all five to the size of the middle cup. She would have to use Augmentation on the smaller cups and Reduction on the larger cups.

Shannon noticed Jax and Darius watching her with apprehensive expressions. She turned her back towards them, not wanting their nerves to add to her own. She closed her eyes and tried to imagine that she was back in the training room at Mabre House.

Holding her breath, Shannon projected the spells one at a time. She didn't start breathing again until all the cups were the same size, taking in a huge gulp of air in relief. Darius started clapping, amazed. The last time he had seen Shannon try these spells, he had nearly lost his favourite pair of shoes because she had made them so tiny they had disappeared down a crack in the floor.

The professor carried on without commenting. She dropped two of the cups onto the stone floor, causing them to smash into several pieces. Shannon, feeling more confident, repaired them easily.

Finally, it was time for the Cleaning Spell. To start with, she was directed to clean the windowsills high up on the walls. These regularly accumulated a layer of dust which was stirred up by all the spells that were used in the training room on a daily basis.

Then Professor Lenora pointed to herself. Shannon paused. She had known that this would be the last spell, but that didn't make the prospect any easier.

She looked at the professor's immaculately arranged hair and the many tiny, perfect buttons that fastened in a line down the front of her black shirt. The thought of ruining that flawless appearance if she messed up the spell was pretty daunting. But she was not going to stop now.

Shannon sent the spinning silver cloud on its way. In a matter of seconds, it was over. Finally, the professor allowed herself to smile. She walked to Shannon and took both her hands. "My sincere congratulations, Shannon," she said, her eyes sparkling. "I am so proud of you."

Shannon beamed. Jax and Darius got up and came to hug her. They began talking excitedly. Now Shannon only had to make one elementary remedy and her basic training would be officially over.

After confirming that Shannon should prepare a Portal Remedy before her next lesson, Professor Lenora left them to it and returned to her room.

Portal Remedies were always necessary for the first few journeys anyone made. Before your body adjusted to it, that one step through the shimmering doorway could drain all your energy.

And if you didn't use a portal for a few weeks or more, your body would forget, and you'd need to use a Portal Remedy again. This meant that every magician on Androva needed to know how to make one.

"Come on," said Jax. "Let's get out of here. We can finally start to make some plans for the Terran school holidays. The Council can't have any objections now!"

Walking back out into sunshine, which was shining straight into their eyes as the sun fell lower in the sky, Shannon felt as if she didn't have a care in the world. Then suddenly she gasped. "What time is it?" she asked, impatiently pushing her sleeve out of the way so that she could see her watch. "Oh no! It's nearly six o'clock!"

"It's OK, don't worry, you can still make it," said Jax firmly. Darius looked at him questioningly, and he quickly told Darius he would explain later. Taking Shannon's arm, he pulled her back into the Seminary.

They ran to the portal room, Shannon nearly stumbling in her haste to descend the winding staircase.

Jax activated the symbols, his Sygnus spinning. The familiar shimmer rose from the spellstation in front of them to create the doorway to Terra. Shannon looked back at Jax for a moment before she stepped through.

"Wednesday afternoon as usual? Four o' clock?"

Jax nodded. Apart from Saturdays, that was the only time he and Shannon could usually meet without her absence arousing suspicion.

Shannon's sister had swimming lessons after school, followed by dinner at her friend's house. The friend's mother was a good friend of Shannon's mother. With her father regularly working late for his promotion, Shannon was usually alone for a few hours and could go to Androva without having to make any excuses.

Shannon hesitated. There was so much they needed to talk about, and she hadn't even had the chance to ask Jax about his Concealing Spell. Then she pictured what her mother's face would look like if she were late.

Looking at Jax apologetically, she mouthed "Thank you..." and, as she stepped backwards though the portal, Androva disappeared.

She ran as fast as she could through the woodland next to her house, and she arrived at the back door out of breath. She kicked off her trainers and ran past her parents, whose expressions were half relieved and half angry.

"I've still got five minutes!" she called down to them on the way to her bedroom. "I'll be ready, I promise!"

She closed her bedroom door and wedged it shut with a small paperback book pushed underneath it, then grabbed the dress she had promised her mother she would wear from the wardrobe. After taking off her jeans and t-shirt, she yanked it over her head.

Then, with a look of concentration on her face, she carefully projected a Cleaning Spell. In less than minute, she looked perfectly neat and tidy. After a quick glance in the mirror, she removed the book that was holding the door shut and ran back downstairs.

Reaching the dining room, where her mother

was putting the finishing touches to the place settings, Shannon tried to adopt a pleasant expression.

Her mother looked her up and down, still very cross, but thankful that Shannon looked so presentable. Just as she opened her mouth to tell Shannon off for arriving home so late, the doorbell rang. Their important guest had arrived.

Shannon's father opened the door, and to Shannon's surprise, she heard the soft, sweet-sounding tones of a woman's voice. Her father had said that his new boss was called Tony Maxwell, and Shannon had assumed that to be a man's name.

As her father reappeared in the doorway, Shannon's jaw dropped. The woman with her father was stunningly beautiful. She had ink-black hair that fell in gentle waves over her shoulders, and vivid blue eyes. Her pale skin was flawless, and her perfect red lips widened in a dazzling smile as she saw Shannon.

Shannon blushed. All of a sudden she was painfully aware of her own unstyled hair, her plain dress in a colour that didn't particularly suit her, and her complete lack of make-up. She wished that she had at least put some lip gloss on or something.

"This is Ms. Toni Maxwell," began her father. He introduced Shannon's mother, and then

Tammy, who was half-hiding behind her mother as she looked in awe at the new arrival. Then it was Shannon's turn to be introduced.

"M-Ms. Maxwell," Shannon stammered.

"Oh, please call me Toni," corrected the woman. She was even lovelier close up, and her perfume smelled like peaches. "It's short for Antoinette, but I prefer Toni."

Shannon's parents made sure that everyone had a drink, and they sat outside in the garden for a little while as the dinner finished cooking.

Shannon tried not to stare at their guest, who really was the most beautiful woman she had ever seen in real life. She seemed to be perfectly sweet and charming as well, and not at all the tough executive that Shannon had been expecting.

Shannon felt herself relaxing. It looked like this evening was not going to be as bad as she had expected. The conversation between Toni and her parents seemed to flow quite naturally, with Shannon able to contribute from time to time without feeling self-conscious. And having passed five out of six disciplines in her year one assessment earlier, it was as if a weight had been lifted off her shoulders. She wanted to smile at everyone.

The garden, her father's pride and joy, was full of plants and flowers blooming in all their summer glory. Heavy pink roses seemed almost too large for their stems to support, and two or three sleepy bees drifted over the purple haze of sweet-smelling lavender around the patio.

Although Shannon was still keeping her force field under careful control, she was surrounded by so much living magic that the energy was making her bare arms tingle and her eyes glitter slightly.

Toni glanced at Shannon, intrigued. Shannon now looked completely different from the slightly awkward teenager who had greeted her earlier.

As they went back into the house for dinner and sat down at the table, Toni spoke to Shannon.

"Tell me about school, Shannon. Which subjects do you and your friends like best?" she asked. "Do you know any science fans that could become InterPharm chemists one day? We like to keep our ears to the ground for future talent," she added with a wink.

Shannon smiled back at her. "I actually quite like science myself," she answered truthfully. Until recently, English and Science had been her favourite subjects. She loved reading, and she loved experimenting. All of that had kind of taken a back seat since becoming a magician though.

"Really?" said Toni, smiling more widely. "Well then, you should come and spend the day at our UK head office so that you can take a closer look at some of our research. I could take you out to lunch and talk to you about our student training programme."

Shannon's heart sank for a moment, while her parents looked at each other in delight. Then she decided to be sensible. If she gave up a day of her summer holidays for the InterPharm visit, her mother was likely to give her more freedom the rest of the time.

"That would be great," she said politely.

Toni handed Shannon her business card and made a note of Shannon's mobile number. "I'll call you," Toni promised. "We're launching our new line of cosmetics in September, so I'll make sure that you get some free samples too."

Shannon brightened. She didn't usually wear a lot of make-up, but she figured that cosmetics advice from Toni couldn't hurt. The woman was drop-dead gorgeous after all. And with beautiful blonde Hesta being so determined to go after Jax, Shannon was feeling a tiny bit insecure about her appearance.

The dinner was a success, with Toni praising the food. While the three adults had coffee, Shannon obligingly helped to clear the table and took Tammy upstairs to get ready for bed.

Then they went back down to say goodbye to their guest. Just before she left, Toni asked

Shannon about the InterPharm values. "Honesty, Respect, and Teamwork," repeated Shannon without hesitation. Her father smiled.

"Very good." Toni nodded approvingly. "But actions speak louder than words. I have no reason to doubt your honesty"—at this Shannon swallowed—"and I'm very pleased to see that you treat your parents with respect. You also demonstrated good teamwork by looking after your sister. I'm very impressed."

She reached in her bag for her car keys, turning to leave, then Tammy spoke up.

"I'm honest too," she said earnestly.

Toni looked back, smiling indulgently. "I'm sure you are, Tammy," she replied. "There should be no secrets in the InterPharm family. Goodnight, everyone."

Tammy frowned. "No secrets?" she checked, looking anxious.

"No secrets," confirmed Toni as Shannon's father opened the door to let her out. "Thank you all for a lovely evening."

Shannon watched the wheels turning in her sister's brain and knew what Tammy was going to say the second before she opened her mouth.

7 Secrets And Rumours

"But I have a secret," blurted out Tammy, at the same moment Shannon said hastily, "Time for bed, Tammy!"

Shannon pulled on her sister's arm, but Tammy dug her heels in. Toni turned back to face them curiously.

"A secret?" she said, and Tammy nodded earnestly. Toni glanced at Shannon, who half shrugged her shoulders, trying desperately to hide her panic. Bending down to Tammy's level, Toni asked, "Do you want to tell me what it is?"

Tammy nodded again, a serious look on her face, while her parents exchanged a puzzled look.

"It's Shannon..." Tammy began. After a dramatic pause, she declared, "She can do magic!"

Shannon's parents laughed. "Alright, Tammy," said her father, putting his hand on his daughter's shoulder. "Toni doesn't have time for your imaginary stories. I think Shannon's right. It's time you went to bed."

"But it's true!" said Tammy, her voice rising. "I saw her do it! I did! There was fairy dust and everything!"

Shannon's parents were starting to look a bit embarrassed. "Sorry about this," said Shannon's father. "I'll take her to bed. See you at the management meeting on Monday morning, Toni."

He picked Tammy up and started to carry her up the stairs.

"It's true, it's true, why won't you believe me?" she wailed tearfully. Shannon lowered her eyes, feeling quite guilty. It was awful for Tammy, but what was Shannon supposed to do?

She could hardly say "Oh yes, I've been a magician for about a month now, and it's really cool, does anyone fancy a demonstration?"

When Shannon raised her eyes again, she found that Toni was looking at her thoughtfully. Shannon tried to brazen it out, hoping that her expression looked convincingly baffled.

After Toni finally left, Shannon helped her mother finish tidying the kitchen. She wanted to keep busy rather than think about what had just happened. Her mother was happy to have the help, and thanked Shannon for being so well behaved that evening.

It seemed to Mrs. Blackwood as if the grumpy, argumentative Shannon of the past few weeks had temporarily disappeared, and she was very grateful to have the old Shannon back.

Finally, Shannon had to go to bed, which meant that she was alone with her own thoughts. Fortunately, after such a long day with so many spells, she was too tired to stay awake for long. Morning arrived before she knew it, and by then she was feeling a lot better.

It turned out to be a rather ordinary day, in stark contrast to what had happened the day before. Penny came round to Shannon's house, and they did their Geography homework together.

Shannon also managed to make up with Tammy, but she insisted that the "magic" Tammy thought she had seen on Friday evening was all in her imagination. She was so firm about it that Tammy eventually stopped protesting.

Penny was full of questions about what had happened on Saturday with the big dinner and Shannon's day with Jax. She was incredulous that Shannon still didn't have a photo of Jax on her phone.

As far as Penny knew, Jax lived in London, and Shannon had met him one weekend while he was in the area visiting his aunt and uncle.

"Get him to send you a selfie now," urged

Penny. "Come on, what's the problem? Has he just had a bad haircut or something?"

"He doesn't have a phone at the moment," answered Shannon, figuring that much at least was true.

Penny gave Shannon a dubious look. "You're not lying to me, are you? It doesn't matter if he's not really hot. I'm not that shallow you know."

Shannon smiled inwardly. You have no idea, she thought. She tried not to make a big deal out of it, because Jax's self-confidence was already bordering on arrogance at times, but there was no doubt that he was amazing-looking.

"I'm not lying to you," she confirmed to Penny. "He really doesn't have a phone."

Then Shannon changed the subject, talking about the dinner, and how unexpectedly beautiful their guest had been. They looked up Toni's photo on the InterPharm website, and Penny agreed that she was pretty stunning.

"For an older woman of course," she qualified.

Soon it was time for Penny to go home, and Shannon decided to get an early night. She was looking forward to trying out the Cleaning Spell before school, and deliberately screwed her uniform up in a heap on the floor to put the spell to the test.

Fortunately, it went like clockwork the following morning, and Shannon walked down early for breakfast, feeling a bit smug.

"What's going on?" asked her mother in mock horror. "Are you ill? An attack of good behaviour lasting this long could be serious. I'd better make you an appointment with the doctor!"

"Ha, ha," replied Shannon, going to get a bowl for her cereal.

"Oh, before I forget," her mother continued, "someone's finally moving into the house across the road today. Your father was nearly blocked in by the moving van when he left for work this morning. That means you can't cut through their garden on your way to and from school anymore."

Shannon looked annoyed.

"Don't give me that face," said her mother. "The SOLD sign has been up outside for over a week, you knew this would happen."

Shannon kicked the table leg irritably. "Yes, but that doesn't mean I have to be happy about it."

"I'll cancel the doctor's appointment then, shall I?" asked her mother with a rueful smile. "Looks like your good behaviour has been officially cured."

Shannon smiled reluctantly. "You never know, I might have another attack later."

She finished her breakfast and was just finding her shoes when Penny arrived at the door. They usually walked to school together in the mornings if Penny was early enough. The two girls crossed the road, avoiding a large puddle left by the overnight rain, and watched the moving van for a moment. A black leather sofa was being manoeuvred to the door of the van by two cheerful-looking removal men.

"I suppose this means we have to go the long way round," said Penny gloomily. "I forgot my umbrella too, and it's probably going to rain any minute." She squinted up at the sky, which was full of ominous grey clouds.

Shannon looked at the house. Though the front door was open and the sofa was halfway through it, there was no sign of the new owner. Penny grabbed her hand. "I dare you."

Shannon's eyes lit up at the challenge. "You're on!" she replied, and they ran down the side of the house and into its rather overgrown garden. When they were halfway to the gate in the back fence, an angry voice shouted at them.

"Stop! What do you think you're doing? Get off my property!"

Shannon looked over her shoulder as she ran, and glimpsed the furious face of a grey-haired man shaking his fist from an upstairs window. The girls didn't stop until they were through the gate and several metres along the path on the other side.

Laughing, they paused for a moment to get their breath back. Suddenly the gate opened and the same man stepped through.

Shannon jumped, and Penny gave a little gasp of shock. How had he caught up with them so fast? His grey hair was cropped close to his head, and his black clothes and irate expression made him look quite threatening.

"Teenagers, I might have known," he barked at them. "If I ever catch you on my land again, I will report you to the police." Walking forward a few paces, he continued. "And if the local police don't punish you, I will."

Penny scowled at him. "You can't do anything to us. That's against the law!"

"Trespassing on private property is against the law too, but that didn't stop you!" spat the man in response.

Then, scowling at them, he walked back through the gate, slamming it behind him and making the fence rattle.

"Well, someone got out of bed on the wrong side this morning!" joked Penny. Shannon tried to smile. She hoped that her parents wouldn't hear about it, because the last thing she needed was to be grounded.

It was a long Monday morning at school, which kicked off as usual with double Maths. Shannon and Penny were in different sets for

Maths, so they didn't meet up again until afterwards. The school buildings looked even greyer than usual under the dark clouds in the sky.

The corridors smelled of unwashed PE clothes and old school dinners, and Shannon thought longingly of the Seminary of Magic. Finally it was lunchtime, and she grabbed a seat in the cafeteria with Penny and their other friends Naomi and Megan.

The noisy chatter of several hundred children combined with the rattle of cutlery as the room filled up. Half-heartedly, the group picked at their shepherd's pie and chips, today's lunch option. They talked about their respective weekends and how utterly boring it was to be back at school.

Naomi complained that her red hair would go frizzy in the rain. Shannon rolled her eyes at Penny. Naomi was always complaining about her hair. Megan applied some new pink lip gloss.

"What's that for?" asked Penny. "Or should I say *who's* that for?" she added slyly. Megan glared at Penny. She had History after lunch, and she would be sitting next to Freddy, a boy she had liked all term, but who showed no signs of asking her out yet.

Naomi's boyfriend, Patrick, had walked up to them while Penny was talking. Stealing a seat from the neighbouring table, he sat down next to

Naomi and draped his arm possessively over the back of her chair. He had scruffy blond hair and a cheeky grin, which widened as he looked at Megan.

"Secret boyfriend?" he asked her.

"None of your business," retorted Megan. "Anyway, it's Shannon who has the secret boyfriend," she continued, to divert Patrick's attention.

Shannon frowned at Megan. "He's not secret, he just doesn't go to *this* rubbish excuse for a school," she countered.

"A mystery man!" said Patrick curiously. "So that's why you won't go out with Leo."

Leo was Patrick's best friend, and he had finally got up the courage to ask Shannon out on a date a few weeks ago. You can hardly blame Shannon for refusing him though.

Leo, with his spiky brown hair and pale blue eyes, was perfectly nice looking. But he wasn't exactly in a position to compete with a black-haired, green-eyed magician from another world.

"No mystery," said Shannon, keeping her tone casual and hoping that someone would change the subject.

"Talking of mystery men," said Patrick, taking out his phone to open a website page.

The girls groaned. "Not another freaky internet rumour," said Penny, shaking her head.

Patrick was known for regularly trying to scare them all with crazy stories he got from a dubious internet site.

Patrick ignored Penny. "I was just reading about this kidnapper who was let out of prison recently. They call him The Magic Man," he said, putting on a spooky voice, "because he's totally obsessed with magic tricks, like sawing people in half and stuff.

"And get this—they gave him a new identity, so no one knows who he is or what he looks like. He could be living next door to any of us!" he finished gleefully, waiting for a reaction.

The girls groaned again. "Is this from the same website that said zombies had escaped from a secret hospital and were walking the streets at night eating people?" said Penny.

"And didn't they say last month that a thousand-year-old dragon had escaped from a dungeon in London?" continued Naomi, laughing.

"And what about the family of ghosts looking for a bloodthirsty revenge after being burned at the stake hundreds of years ago?" added Shannon.

"You may laugh," replied Patrick, looking offended. "But you'll be sorry if it turns out to be true. If a man all dressed in black moved in next door to me, I would make sure the doors to the house were well and truly locked."

Shannon and Penny looked at each other, remembering the man who had shouted at them that very morning.

"A man dressed in black?" asked Shannon.

"Yeah, he only wears black, because then the blood doesn't show," said Patrick nonchalantly.

Naomi made a face. "Remind me again why I like you?" she said.

The bell rang for the end of lunchtime, and everyone got up from the table. As they walked back to their classrooms, Penny grabbed Shannon by the arm and whispered to her, "You don't think…?"

8 The Binding Spell

Shannon knew what Penny was asking. "No, I don't," she said firmly. She was not going to give space in her head to Patrick's crazy story. "You didn't believe in the zombies, the dragon, or the ghosts, did you?"

Penny shook her head, feeling a bit silly. "No, of course not," she answered.

Following afternoon registration, their form teacher, Mr. Andrews, clapped his hands for silence.

"I have a favour to ask you," he began, pushing his glasses up his rather pointed nose. Shannon noticed that there was a hole in one of the sleeves of his grey cardigan.

"Next week is the last week of term before the summer holidays," he continued, and there was a small cheer and some laughter from the back of the classroom.

"Thank you, Mr. Stone," said the teacher to

one of the boys at the back, "we all know how disappointed *you* will be when school finishes." There was more laughter.

"As you know, we are hosting our traditional open day for new students who will be joining us later this September. Unfortunately, the enthusiasm of years ten and eleven to participate is less than we might have hoped. We need two more volunteers to represent the school."

Shannon was only half listening. She was thinking about Jax's Concealing Spell and wondering what was so difficult about it.

"Anyone?" pressed Mr. Andrews.

Suddenly Shannon had a flash of inspiration. "We'll do it!" she called, holding up her hand and Penny's with it.

"What?" hissed Penny. "Are you crazy?"

"Thank you, Shannon," responded Mr. Andrews, "I'll put your names on the list."

The class broke up to go to afternoon lessons, and Penny turned to Shannon, annoyed. "What did you do that for?" she asked.

Shannon grinned, looking pleased with herself. "You'll see," she replied. "It'll be brilliant. I'll explain later. Just trust me, and I promise you'll agree."

"You'd better be telling the truth," Penny muttered.

Shannon's grin grew even wider. I think I just

had an idea how Jax and Darius can visit my school, she thought. She couldn't wait until Wednesday when she could tell them about it.

Jax, meanwhile, was hoping that Wednesday wouldn't arrive too quickly. He wanted to get his Concealing Spell over and done with before then. He had decided that Shannon seeing him wearing pink, even if it was only on his shoulder, was just not an option.

Unfortunately, things were not exactly going to plan. It was approaching Monday evening, and Jax still hadn't managed to keep the pink monstrosity on top of his Sygnus for more than half an hour at a time. Whenever he started worrying about what people would think of him, the energy of the spell vibrated and then dissolved.

Darius at first thought it was hilarious, and what was worse, he had already managed to complete his own Concealing Spell. Admittedly, Darius had only been required to cover his Sygnus with a piece of plain cloth. But knowing that his friend had beaten him had put Jax in an incredibly bad mood.

Having realised that his laughter was not helping, Darius tried to be more constructive, but his advice wasn't being very well received. They were in the training room at Mabre House, and the pink square of fabric had just slithered unceremoniously to the floor for the third time. There it sat, glowing like a neon sign, until Jax kicked it irritably towards the far wall.

"Perhaps the spell needs a different kind of magic than you've been using?" Darius suggested tentatively. "Something less forceful maybe?" It was rare for Darius to perform better than Jax when learning a new spell, but not unheard of. Jax's style of magic was bold, brash, and fast, whereas Darius took a more steady, measured approach.

If you were to touch their respective magical force fields, you would be able to feel it. Imagine putting your hand under the tumbling rapids of a waterfall. The pressure and energy would be intense, like Jax's magic. Then imagine putting your hand into a deep, still pool of water. It would feel smooth and calm, like Darius's magic. Some spells were better suited to one type than another.

Darius didn't dare suggest that the spell was too difficult, but privately he thought that the more annoyed Jax got, the less likely he was going to be successful. Jax looked at him scornfully.

"A *different* kind of magic?" he repeated mockingly. Grabbing hold of his grey shirt sleeve, he tore off part of the material with an angry rip, then he filled it with the Concealing Spell. He placed it over his Sygnus, and the spell dropped into place at once. Jax looked accusingly at Darius.

"I can do the spell," he said through gritted teeth. "It's the method that's the problem."

"Why does it matter whether Shannon or anyone else sees you anyway?" Darius asked. "You were going to ask for her help two days ago, and now you're acting like it would be the end of the world if she sees you."

Jax ground his gritted teeth together. A part of him knew he was behaving like a spoiled brat, but he hadn't realised quite how embarrassing he would find the spell until he actually saw himself in the mirror.

It is not that Jax wasn't overreacting a bit, because he was. But he was also facing something of a challenge.

For an Androvan teenager to wear pink would be similar to a Terran teenager walking around dressed in extravagant clown make-up. Something completely crazy and unexpected, that you would never normally see. Red nose, painted face, big fluffy wig—the lot.

Jax fully understood now that for the first time in his life, he would have to forget all about his pride and his ego. He was too ashamed to admit, even to Darius, that he didn't know if he could do it.

Darius, giving up, went home for dinner, leaving Jax alone with his thoughts. Jax slept badly, and awoke the following day in an even worse mood than before. The morning at the Seminary passed very slowly.

At the start of the afternoon, Jax was in a Living Magic class with Professor Lenora, the Seminary's expert professor in that particular discipline. The challenge for that afternoon's lesson was to harvest living magic from a healthy plant and transfer it to a less healthy one.

This was not something that had ever been done before. Living magic could be filled with spells, and used by magicians to temporarily boost their own ability. But it could not be returned to the source once harvested.

Trees and plants naturally grew back their magic over time, and were a little weaker until this was completed.

The reason for this afternoon's experimental lesson was to try to fix a problem outside the city in the cultivation fields. Androva was very dependent on its crops to feed everyone, and there were early signs that the fruit harvest that summer was going to be poor. This could cause Androva a big problem in the coming winter.

At first it had seemed as if only a few plants were affected, but now leaves were turning brown all over the place, and people were getting

ALEX C VICK

worried. The Council had therefore asked the Seminary professors to explore new spells, with the aim of healing the damaged fruit-bearing plants and trees before it was too late.

There were some experiments being managed by Professor Alver in Manipulation, and Professor Jonas was trying to create some new remedies that might help. And of course, Professor Lenora was in charge of the Living Magic research.

Underage magicians were very good at harvesting living magic, much better than older magicians. The coming of age ceremony, held at the end of each magician's eighteenth year, fixed their magical ability forever. The intention was to prevent any one magician becoming too powerful. This meant that older magicians usually found it more difficult to collect additional magic.

On any other day, Jax would have been delighted to be trying out new spells. It was one of his favourite pastimes. But he sat with his arms folded and a scowl on his face. Darius, sitting next to him, sighed with exasperation.

"Lighten up," he whispered to his friend. "It's not the end of the world if you can't do it. Why don't you ask Professor Alver for some help?"

Jax glared at Darius and opened his mouth to argue. Before he could speak, Professor Lenora looked across at the two boys, raising one perfectly arched eyebrow.

"Jax, Darius, would you care to share your conversation with the rest of us? If you are going to be so rude as to interrupt my class, you must have some real words of wisdom to impart."

Darius immediately apologised, while Jax continued to glower. The professor waited.

"Apologise or don't apologise, I don't really care one way or the other, Jax," she said evenly. "But when you can't open the portal for Shannon's next visit because you're writing an essay on Cultivation Spells for me…"

Jax felt his temper rise several notches higher. I saved you all! he wanted to shout. I was the one who carried out the Spell of Removal on Angelus! ME! You're all treating me like I'm still a child!

He jumped up out of his chair, turning it over in his anger, and stormed out of the room. The other underage magicians watched him go with a mixture of horror and excitement. Disobedience at the Seminary was very rare.

No one wanted to be subjected to a Binding Spell, which was the traditional punishment for breaking the rules. It temporarily smothered your magical force field. The spell was only used at the Seminary on underage magicians, and only professors (and former professors) knew how to do it. It usually worked as a very effective deterrent.

The class turned to the professor, eager to see how she would handle it. Professor Lenora took a slow breath, her face remaining calm.

"Alright," she said, half to herself and half to her students. "This was always a possibility." Raising her voice, she addressed the underage magicians in front of her. "Please wait here quietly for a moment while I fetch a custodian."

Disappointed that the professor was remaining so composed, her audience whispered amongst themselves. Darius looked unhappy. He wanted to go after Jax himself, but he figured there was no point both of them getting into trouble. At least this way, maybe he would be allowed to open the portal for Shannon the following day if Jax couldn't.

Lenora walked briskly along the corridor outside the training room, her soft shoes making no sound on the black stone floor. She was headed towards the main offices.

As she reached the centre of the H, approaching the entrance, she saw Jax pacing back and forth. His anger had only propelled him this far. Some instinct of self-preservation had stopped him from actually leaving the Seminary. He looked up as he saw the professor.

"Jax…" she started cautiously. She could see from his expression that he was going to be difficult to reason with. Behind Jax, Professor Alver appeared, his eyes widening in surprise to see Jax and Professor Lenora. Jax's fists were clenched, and his entire posture radiated anger.

"Jax," Professor Lenora tried again, "can we talk about this?"

"About what?" replied Jax accusingly. "About how it's necessary for me to make myself a laughing stock before you allow me to learn what I need to know?"

"You misunderstand the purpose of the task that Professor Alver has set you," she replied calmly.

"No I don't!" said Jax, his voice rising. "I understand it perfectly! Is this my reward for saving Androva? Humiliation? Even if I do the spell, and Alver shows me how to build the stupid portal room, Shannon will already have run a mile after seeing me like that!"

He took a step forwards, his hands glowing. He wasn't actually planning to project a spell at Professor Lenora. He just wanted to lash out at the unfairness of it all. Professor Lenora glanced at Professor Alver and nodded her head very slightly.

Alver raised his hands, and before Jax knew what was happening, the Binding Spell had surrounded him. For a few seconds, he struggled against it, but it was like trying to grab hold of fog. It swirled through his magical force field, weighing it down until Jax felt utterly exhausted.

He half turned to see who had projected the spell, and he laughed bitterly. "I might have known," he said. "Are you happy now? I'm sure the Council will be delighted to hear that I've failed. Especially my father."

He put out his hand and leaned against the wall to steady himself. Now that the spell had fully taken hold, Jax was starting to feel as if he could lay down and sleep for a hundred years.

"You can all go back to your rules and regulations, and never worry about Terra again. Well, I hope you enjoy the safe and boring little world you've created." He paused, then added with one final effort, "Actually, forget that. I hope you choke on it."

Worn out, he slid down the wall and closed his eyes.

9 The Concealing Spell Explained

On Wednesday, at five minutes to four o' clock, Shannon was waiting in the woods for the portal to open. She was so excited about her news that she was already smiling in anticipation of Jax's reaction.

The Open Day was the perfect opportunity for Jax and Darius to learn what a Terran school was like, spend the whole day with Shannon, and meet Penny into the bargain.

It wouldn't be nearly so noticeable that they looked and sounded different. It was taken for granted that kids from other schools could be a bit weird sometimes. Not that Jax and Darius were weird, you understand, but... if you met a magician without *knowing* that they were a magician... well, they might seem a bit weird.

Finally Shannon saw the tell-tale shimmer

rising in the air in front of her. She stepped through confidently, accustomed to the sudden change from bright daylight to the dark underground portal room.

Suddenly she realised something was wrong. This was a different portal room from the one in Mabre House. What was going on? Where was Jax?

She turned in a circle, trying to identify her surroundings, and jumped in surprise as she noticed someone standing to her left. It was Professor Alver, who quickly stepped forward to introduce himself.

He was unable to completely conceal his curiosity at finally meeting the underage Terran magician who had fought so bravely on behalf of Androva. He smiled at Shannon with genuine enthusiasm while looking her up and down. She smiled back a little uncertainly.

"You're Jax's professor, aren't you?" she checked. "The one who's going to teach him how to build a portal room for me."

He nodded. "I am," he replied. "At least, that was the plan." He paused, his face becoming serious. "We might have to make a new plan now."

Shannon frowned, waiting for the professor to continue, but there was silence. "Look, I don't mean to be rude, but what's going on?" she asked. "Where is Jax?"

"You can see Jax in a little while," he replied. There was silence again.

Shannon looked at him suspiciously. "Is this some kind of game we're playing here?" she challenged. "Why aren't you giving me any information? Has something happened to Jax? Is he OK?"

Professor Alver regarded her carefully. After Jax's recent behaviour, he and Professor Lenora were trying to manage the consequences between them without involving the Council. They both thought Jax deserved a second chance, but agreed that this was only possible if Shannon didn't leap to his defence.

If both Jax and Shannon started defying the Code together, things could very quickly escalate out of control. Lenora had told him what she had seen of Shannon's ability, and it was off the charts.

"I need to know that I can trust you," he began. "And I don't mean trust you to keep a secret. I mean can I trust you to hear this with your head rather than your heart?"

His expression was sincere, and Shannon calmed down a bit.

"It depends on what you're going to say," she replied honestly. "But I promise to give my head the chance to catch up with my heart *before* I go crazy on you, if that's any help?" she continued with a slightly mischievous grin.

Alver chuckled despite himself. "Fair enough," he said. He began to describe the events of the previous day, but Shannon interrupted him, asking about the exact conditions of the Concealing Spell. Jax had never got the chance to tell her about it. As the professor elaborated, Shannon sighed.

"I can guess what happened," she responded. "But tell me anyway."

The professor continued, finishing by telling her that Jax had spent the night at the Seminary until the Binding Spell wore off so that Revus would not need to know about it.

"He can't laugh at himself," Shannon said ruefully, shaking her head. "You asked him to do the impossible."

Professor Alver stared at her in surprise. "I have to confess we expected you to take his side," he said.

"I am on his side. I think Jax is awesome." A small smile broke through her solemn expression. "He's a brilliant magician. Don't tell him I said that!" she added hastily. Alver tried to hide his amusement. He was starting to like this Terran girl. "But his sense of humour is definitely a work in progress," she continued.

Alver looked at Shannon for a moment. He

finally relaxed the glow of the Containment Spell that he had been projecting as far as his fingertips in readiness all this time. He gestured to the foot of the staircase, and they began to climb to the surface.

Shannon's mind was spinning. Despite the fact that she had told the truth to Professor Alver just now, she was still really worried about Jax, and she thought the spell had been unfair. She wasn't going to launch an attack at anyone in retaliation, but she was going to help Jax find a way to do the spell if it was the last thing she did.

It's partly my fault anyway, she thought. If I hadn't left early on Saturday, this might not have happened. She followed Professor Alver with a determined expression.

Jax was waiting for them in the living area upstairs. They were in Professor Alver's house some way outside of the centre of the city. He lived alone, as did most of the Seminary professors.

Teaching on Androva was a big commitment in terms of time and effort, and few professors had time for anything else. Shannon noticed that the house was a good size, with mostly red and green furnishings. They reminded her a little of Christmas decorations.

As Shannon came into the room, Jax turned away with an obstinate expression, and for a moment she feared he was angry with her. With a self-conscious glance at Professor Alver, she went over to Jax and put her hand on his arm.

Jax didn't move. His arm muscles were stiff and unyielding under Shannon's hand. He was scared that she was going to laugh at him, or even worse, break up with him. But he didn't want to show that he cared. At least he wouldn't give her the satisfaction of seeing that.

"Hey," she said softly. Jax kept his head turned away. "Look at me," she pleaded. Jax turned his head very slightly towards her, but would not meet her eyes. She stood on tiptoe and whispered in his ear.

"I don't care if you have to dress in pink from head to toe," she began. Jax's eyes widened in disbelief. "I don't care if you have pink eyelashes and pink fingernails," she continued.

Jax raised his eyebrows as he pictured this.

"I don't care if you have pink teeth, and pink earrings in the shape of Jelly Babies."

Jax couldn't prevent a breath of laughter from escaping him, and his arms went round Shannon's body in a hug. She felt him relax as she hugged him back.

Professor Alver watched them, relieved that Jax's anger seemed to be dissipating, but wishing he knew what Shannon had whispered to Jax to change his mood so quickly. The two underage magicians turned back to face the professor, holding hands. Jax apologised to Professor Alver, the first time he had done so with sincerity since the Binding Spell.

The professor offered them a drink, asking if they would stay for a while so that he could get to know Shannon a bit better. They moved into the kitchen, sitting on wooden chairs that were covered with red and green striped cushions.

Shannon explained about her school's Open Day the following week. Her earlier excitement started to return as she talked, and she became more animated.

"Isn't it perfect?" she finished happily. "I've nearly passed my year one assessment, so the Council should agree that it's safe. It will make the summer holidays much easier too, because I can say that I met Jax and Darius at the Open Day. My parents won't be worried that I just met some random weirdo on the internet or something. Everyone will be totally chilled about it."

Jax looked at the professor for a second, and got an equally perplexed look in return. Though they had understood the meaning of what Shannon was saying, some of her actual words were completely unfamiliar. Jax remembered Shannon mentioning something about an internet, but he didn't really get it yet.

ALEX C VICK

"What?" asked Shannon, grinning. "Too many Terran words for you?"

She giggled at their expressions. Professor Alver smiled. "Though I would love to know more about where you come from, Shannon, I think the world of the Terran teenager is a step too far for me," he said, shaking his head.

Jax wasn't put off. Yes, he was a bit nervous about finally going to Terra in daylight, but at the same time, it was really exciting. As a magic-taker, he had only been allowed to visit at night, and never to stay for longer than necessary. Now he would actually be able to take part in Terran life.

It would be like walking into one of the fiction books he had recently begun to read and temporarily living a different life.

"So what do you think?" Shannon asked Professor Alver. "Can we ask the Council?"

The professor nodded. "I don't see why not. Although Professor Lenora and I would feel more reassured if Jax mastered the Concealing Spell first."

Jax's face fell and he looked down at the floor. For a moment, while his head was full of dreams of Terra, he had forgotten the spell. Shannon looked at him sympathetically. When he lifted his head back up, though, his face was calm. "Can I ask you something?" he said to the professor.

"Of course," came the reply.

"Professor Lenora told me that I had misunderstood the purpose of the spell," Jax said. "Can you tell me what she meant?"

Alver nodded. "I tried to explain it to you at the time," he began. "In challenging you to carry out this particular spell, I was paying you a huge compliment."

Jax opened his mouth to disagree, but then thought better of it and remained silent.

"There are very few magicians who can perform spells against themselves in this way. Probably less than fifty on the whole of Androva. I am one of them," he continued matter-of-factly. "Your father is another."

Jax opened his mouth again, this time in shock.

"There is no accepted test for an underage magician to demonstrate whether he or she has this ability," explained the professor. "This is because no underage magician has ever been considered worthy of such a test before. And so I had to design one especially for you."

Jax considered this for a moment. "You're telling me the truth?" he asked finally. "You're not just trying to make me feel better?"

Professor Alver laughed. "I do indeed hope that you feel better, but that doesn't mean I'm not telling you the truth as well. I had wanted you to figure this out for yourself, based on the information I gave you. One of your biggest weaknesses is your pride, Jax," he added gently. "If you can't overcome it, you will never reach your full potential."

Jax felt annoyed again, but only with himself this time. "You must think I'm pretty ridiculous," he muttered.

"No," corrected the professor. "For what it's worth, I do not. And neither does Professor Lenora. But you should not waste time concerning yourself with what we think. You should focus on mastering the spell."

Jax stood up, taking a deep breath. "I will," he said. "I want to get started on it right now."

Alver shook his head slightly. "The Binding Spell will not have completely worn off yet," he warned. "If I were you I would wait until tomorrow."

Then he suggested that they open a portal to Mabre House and spend some time together before Shannon had to return home. He mentioned that there would be a Council meeting on Saturday, which would be the perfect time to ask permission for Jax and Darius's trip to Terra the following week.

"I'm not saying that I won't support the trip if you don't carry out the spell," Professor Alver told Jax. "But you have to convince me that you've tried."

Jax nodded. Shannon got up to stand next to him. "We can still talk about it, even if you can't practice yet," she told him. "Anyway, I've got an idea…"

10 Revus Remembers Arianna

Professor Alver watched them go, feeling much more reassured than he had before Shannon's arrival. He was looking forward to telling Professor Lenora, knowing that she had also been nervous about the chance they had both taken by not involving the Council.

When Jax and Shannon arrived at Mabre House, they went to the training room so that he could show her the pink material. Shannon exclaimed when she saw it, picking it up and turning it over in her hands.

"This is totally disgusting," she agreed. "It's mesmerising, but not in a good way. Is there a spell in it or something? I hate it, but I can't take my eyes off it."

Jax was a bit relieved. "So you don't think I was overreacting then?" he asked.

Shannon shook her head. "No, I get why this would be a problem," she replied. "I'm not sure I could wear it, and I have a head start on you. Not just because I'm a girl, but because people on Terra do wear some seriously bizarre stuff sometimes."

Then she looked him in the eyes. "But refusing to do the spell is one thing. Storming out of class and attacking a professor might be taking it a bit far."

"I didn't actually attack her!" countered Jax.

There was a short silence. "Look, I know I was an idiot," admitted Jax. "What do you want me to say? I can't change what happened now."

"What was it like?" Shannon asked curiously. "The Binding Spell, I mean."

Jax thought for a moment. "Like being helpless," he replied. "The worst feeling ever."

He opened his hands and looked down at them as he projected the glow of his force field outwards. Though he was feeling much better, the professor had been right. He was not back to normal.

"What was your idea then?" Jax asked, putting his hands back down. "If we both agree that pink thing is beyond hideous, then how can I possibly do the spell?"

Shannon smiled. "Have you ever heard of the expression 'so bad it's good'?" she said.

Jax shook his head. "That doesn't make any sense," he replied.

Shannon laughed. "I think it's about time we shook up the world of underage magic a bit," she said. "We're going to start a new craze."

Jax looked at her in bewilderment, and she started to explain.

"Teenagers can be a bit unoriginal sometimes," she began. "I bet that it's no different on Androva. You see these words on my T-shirt?"

She pointed to the burgundy lettering which stood out boldly against the white of the cotton material. Next to the letters, in the same colour, was the silhouette of a bird.

"These letters make this T-shirt cool," she continued. "So I wear this T-shirt because it makes me look more cool too."

"Says who?" questioned Jax. "I mean, do those letters actually mean anything?"

"Not really," said Shannon, smiling. "Don't tell my mum, because this T-shirt costs a lot more with these letters on it. But that's not the point."

"So what *is* the point?" asked Jax.

"The point is that people, especially people our age, will do anything to be cool. And you're going to make them believe that pink thing is cool."

Jax looked at her sceptically. "Really? And exactly how am I going to do that?"

Shannon beckoned him closer, her brown eyes

full of mischief. "Kiss me, and I'll tell you," she promised.

All too soon, it was time for Shannon to return home. After climbing back up the portal room stairs, Jax realised he was starving. He and Shannon had been so busy making plans for the Concealing Spell that they had forgotten to have any dinner.

He made himself some bread and cheese before heading back to his room to see if he was strong enough to practice the spell yet. Fortunately, Revus was still at work, so Jax didn't have to answer any questions about his unexpected overnight stay at the Seminary.

Sitting on the windowsill, he looked out across the countryside towards the mountain. The setting sun was turning the sky gold. A few figures were still visible in one of the fruit fields, despite the lateness of the hour.

Belatedly he remembered the Living Magic lesson of the day before, and what Professor Lenora had been telling them about the dying plants. But his thoughts soon turned back to the Concealing Spell.

His force field still seemend different. Jax felt as if his magic were only half awake. He concentrated, starting at the centre of his mind, where his initial spark of magic still glowed as brightly as ever.

But when he tried to draw his magic back together, as he would if he were defending himself against a Scattering Spell, nothing happened.

Frustrated, he stopped for a moment. There must be a way, he thought. He gazed round the room, looking for inspiration, but not finding anything. Then he leaned his head back against the window and noticed the ceiling. He jumped up in excitement at the sight of the unfinished spells swirling above him.

But how to get to them? He tried using Solo Transference to lift himself up, but at the moment he wasn't strong enough to rise that far. He considered the bookcase, which stretched nearly all the way to the top of the wall on the far side of the room. It had to be worth a try.

With determination, he began to climb. Although his physical strength was diminished, it was not by nearly as much as his magical ability.

When you become a magician on Androva, usually during your thirteenth year, it takes time for that first spark to create a force field. Then it takes more time after that for the force field to become part of you. The process isn't fully completed until the coming of age ceremony some five years later.

After that, you and your magic are pretty much inseparable. But Jax, as a relatively young magician, was still able to climb the bookcase, even while his force field was weak. His physical strength and his magical strength were not completely joined yet.

He was nearly at the top, and starting to reach out for the nearest spell, which was almost in his grasp, when there was a knock at his bedroom door.

Jax, taken completely by surprise, lost his grip on the bookcase and fell to the floor with an almighty crash. About twenty books fell down as well, most of them unfortunately landing on top of him.

"Jax?" said Revus, throwing open the door when he heard the noise. "What on Androva do you think you're…" His voice trailed off as he saw the books everywhere and Jax gingerly pushing himself up into a sitting position.

"It's not what it looks like," started Jax, immediately on the defensive as he saw his father. Then he realised how ridiculous he sounded. What excuse could he possibly give?

Meeting Revus's astonished gaze, he started to giggle helplessly. After a long pause, and to Jax's amazement, Revus began to laugh as well. He walked forward and offered his hand to help Jax stand up.

"Are you alright?" Revus asked.

"I think so," replied Jax, brushing himself

down.

"I don't suppose there's any point in me asking what you were doing climbing the bookcase?" said Revus. He looked at Jax, hopeful that their shared laughter might mean that his son would be prepared to talk to him for once.

Jax considered. His first instinct had been to ask Revus to leave his room. But it didn't make sense to be stand-offish, after Revus had seen him sprawled across the floor in such an undignified way. And so, for the first time in a very long time, he asked his father to stay.

"Do you promise you won't be mad?" Jax started.

Revus frowned, then tried to smooth the frown away. "I will do my best," he responded.

Jax sighed. Trusting his father was not something that came naturally to him. "It's kind of a long story. Do you know about the Concealing Spell that Alver set me last week?"

Revus shook his head. Jax was surprised. He had thought that the Council would know all about it. He hesitated, wondering if he should tell Revus after all.

Revus leaned forward. "Professor Alver's teaching is between you and him. And as long as it doesn't break the Code, I give you my word that I will not use the information against you."

So Jax told him. Revus would know about it

soon enough anyway, when Jax started walking around wearing his flamboyant pink accessory. Revus sat back in shock. "This is not just a Concealing Spell," he said. "This sounds like a Paradox Spell."

"What?" Jax asked. "A Paradox Spell? That's not how Alver described it."

"Maybe not," replied Revus, "but that's what it is."

"Tell me," Jax pressed. "What is a Paradox Spell? I've never heard of it before."

"It's about mind over matter," explained Revus. "Usually for a spell to work, your mind and your emotions and your physical body have to be united. You see, your magical ability is only an extension of you. You can't naturally perform a spell which would create a contradiction."

"Give me an example," prompted Jax, edging closer to his father in his eagerness to know more. "Alver only told me about performing a spell against myself, or something."

"That is one way to describe it," agreed Revus. "This Concealing Spell will create an outcome that your mind, emotions, and even your physical body will fight against. That is a contradiction. Your magic would not normally be able to work under those conditions."

Jax nodded as he considered this. He remembered how the spell had seemed to dissolve whenever he imagined being ridiculed. And his body had even shrunk backwards slightly as the pink material settled on his shoulder.

"There are several ways in which a similar paradox could be created. You cannot use your magic properly while your physical body is incapacitated somehow," Revus continued.

"And the spells used by Council members during interrogation are designed to disrupt your emotions, which also weakens your ability to use magic."

Jax and Revus exchanged a slightly uncomfortable look, both remembering that Jax had been subjected to interrogation on more than one occasion.

"And you cannot carry out a Combat Spell on yourself," Revus carried on. "That is probably the ultimate Paradox Spell." He paused. "If you can master a Paradox Spell, it means that your magic is unrestricted. No matter what happens to your emotions or your physical body."

"Why would Alver think that I could do a Paradox Spell?" Jax wondered aloud.

"Because of Angelus," Revus replied immediately.

"What?" said Jax, sitting back in shock. He and Revus had never really talked about what had happened since the night itself. He was completely taken aback that Revus would mention it now, and in such a matter-of-fact way.

"What you did..." Revus began, his face softening a little. "You must have been afraid. Maybe even terrified. And yet you still performed the Spell of Removal. Which is like the kind of contradiction I've been describing."

Jax tried not to give the cruel face of Angelus space to reappear inside his head, but was not entirely successful. Then he brightened. That means I can probably do the Concealing Spell after all, he thought. Mind over matter, just like before.

"Thank you," he said, reaching over to touch his father's arm, and Revus gave him a small smile. Seeing the smile, Jax dared to add, "I don't suppose you know how to get rid of the after-effects of a Binding Spell, do you?"

Revus's face immediately closed up again.

"I'm sorry," said Jax hastily, mentally kicking himself. "I shouldn't have asked."

Revus sighed, and a look of such pain came over his face, that Jax involuntarily reached out his arm again, wanting to comfort his father. "You are so much like your mother," Revus said with an effort. He closed his eyes, remembering.

"Arianna treated the rules just like you do. As if they were something that didn't necessarily apply to her."

Jax held his breath. Revus *never* talked about

his mother.

"She was so full of life, and so beautiful." Revus opened his eyes again and looked at Jax. "I never experienced a Binding Spell while I was at the Seminary, but she did. More than once."

He half smiled as he thought of it. "Her curiosity was always getting her into trouble. She figured out how to reverse the Binding Spell after the third time. It turned out to be much easier than either of us expected. I have no doubt that she would pass that information on to you if she were here."

Jax waited, a look of amazement on his face. Revus stood up.

"So, just this once, I will ignore my better judgement. You have only to drink a Portal Remedy, and everything will return to normal," he said. Then he left the room.

Jax sat where he was on the windowsill for a long time, hardly able to believe what had just happened. Then, eventually, he went to bed and dreamed about his mother as an underage magician.

11 Pink Redefined

"When are you going to tell me why we're doing this stupid thing?" demanded Penny on Friday morning on the walk to school. Her long brown hair was tied up in a complicated series of plaits threaded with pink and silver ribbons, and she was wearing a lot of black eyeliner.

"You know Mr. Andrews will send you to wash that off," Shannon pointed out.

"He might not," retorted Penny, "and don't change the subject. We're nearly at the end of term, which means all we should be doing next week is watching semi-educational DVDs while the teachers try to stay awake.

"This is my favourite part of school," she said, completely serious. "But you've signed me up to show round a group of random losers instead!"

Shannon hesitated as they passed her new neighbour's house. They were now walking the long way round, which meant following the path behind his garden fence from its beginning rather than cutting through. Was she imagining it, or was that him watching them from the same upstairs window?

She speeded up, and Penny had to break into a run to catch up with her. "*Shannon!*" she protested.

"Look," Shannon began when they were out of sight of the man's house, "I'll tell you, but it's not definite yet. Jax is still trying to sort things out at his end."

"Jax?" Penny said with a puzzled look. "What's Jax got to do with it?"

Then she realised. "*Jax* is coming to the Open Day?" she asked excitedly. "I finally get to meet Mr. Perfect?"

Shannon grinned. "Hopefully. And he might be bringing his friend Darius too."

"Well, that's more like it!" said Penny with an answering grin. "This Darius, what does he look like? Is he seeing anyone? Do you think he'll like me? Do you think I'll like him?"

"That's a lot of questions," protested Shannon, laughing. "Which one do you want me to answer first?"

Penny linked her arm with Shannon's, and they continued on their way to school, talking nineteen to the dozen as they made plans for the following week. Shannon's thoughts returned to

Jax many times during the school day, as she wondered how he was getting on with his Concealing Spell. She hardly slept that night, and by the time she was waiting for the portal to open on Saturday morning, she was tired and nervous.

She needn't have worried. As soon as she stepped through the portal, she was lifted off her feet and swung round in a big hug by Jax.

"It's working!" he said excitedly into her ear. "Your idea, it's totally working!"

As he set her down, she stepped back, looking to see whether he was wearing the pink square over his Sygnus. It was there, turned on its side so that it formed a diamond shape. As they had agreed, Jax had worn his blackest shirt, so that the pink would show up to dazzling effect.

In the centre of the diamond, Jax had added the letter P, in a curved silver font. Alver had not told him that he couldn't add to the fabric, and Shannon had reasoned that because they were not making it any less ostentatious, it would probably be allowed.

"Why did you choose the letter P in the end?" asked Shannon. She and Jax had discussed a few ideas about how to make the pink fabric look more like a logo, but they had been thinking he would use the letter J.

"It stands for Paradox Spell," said Jax, proceeding to tell Shannon all about the extraordinary conversation he had had with his father on Wednesday evening.

"No one else knows that apart from Darius, and now you," he finished. "I thought if I had a genuinely cool reason for choosing that letter, it might help me. Even though I'm keeping it a secret, I know that it means something amazing. And people are going crazy trying to figure out what it stands for!" he added elatedly.

Shannon smiled back at him, catching his excitement.

"It's really working then?" she checked. "You're OK with it and Professor Alver agrees that you've succeeded?"

Jax nodded. "Don't get me wrong, it was still almost impossible in the beginning," he clarified. "Thursday morning, when I tried the spell before I went to the Seminary, it dissolved again. I was just too scared of what those first few looks would be like, and of what people would think of me."

Shannon gave him a sympathetic look. They had both known that the first few hours would be the hardest.

"I never realised before how difficult it is to do a spell that you genuinely don't want to do," he added, shaking his head. "I don't mean like when you're bored in a lesson, or you'd rather be playing Time Trial. I mean when every single part of you is resisting, but you somehow have to convince your magic to do it anyway."

"But you did it," prompted Shannon. "So you must have figured out a way?"

"Yes," agreed Jax. "I had to detach from what I was feeling, otherwise I couldn't hold the spell." Then he smiled at her. "But I only had the nerve to persevere because of our plan," he said.

"And now it's been way longer than I needed to wear this, but I'm carrying on because it's really funny seeing other underage magicians trying to copy it. It's probably not a proper Paradox Spell now anyway, because I want to do it."

A small alarm bell had gone off in Shannon's head at the thought of Jax being able to completely detach from his emotions. When facing Angelus, they had both overcome their terror to carry out the necessary spells. There had been no time to think about it. Hearing Jax mention that this time he had deliberately and successfully stepped away from his emotions sounded a bit scary.

But seeing how happy he was, she decided to ignore it, and hoped that it would be a long time before he ever had to do another Paradox Spell.

They climbed the stairs, heading for the kitchen. Shannon still needed to make a Portal Remedy to complete her year one assessment.

Although she had created several while back on
Terra out of fruit juice, and tried them herself,
the clear base liquid used for remedies on
Androva was a bit different. So Shannon wanted
to create a proper, traditional Portal Remedy
before taking it to Professor Lenora.

She was fairly certain it would be OK though.
She had even given a few sips of her fruit juice
version to Tammy when she had been tired and
grumpy one morning. Tammy had then bounced
around like a smiling jack-in-the-box all morning,
with no apparent ill effects. (Not counting Mrs.
Blackwood's tiredness after dealing with her
excitable youngest daughter).

Jax watched as Shannon prepared the remedy.
The clear liquid that was the foundation of every
remedy on Androva was extracted from their
domina fruit. This was a bit like the Terran
peach, except with dark purple skin on its
outside.

Carefully Shannon filled her magic with the
spell, and then allowed twenty glowing silver
droplets to fall from the end of her fingertips into
the liquid. Once the remedy was ready, in its slim
blue bottle, they decided to take it to the
Seminary straight away.

"Let's walk," suggested Jax with a grin, "and
see if we can spread the word about my new logo
a bit more." Shannon agreed.

They didn't get too far before a pair of underage magicians noticed him and nudged each other. They looked like they were trying (and failing) to get up the courage to speak to Jax and Shannon. Eventually Jax took pity on them and beckoned them over.

"You're Jax, aren't you?" asked the girl. "I mean, obviously you are," she babbled nervously. "I've seen you around, and everyone's heard about what you both did." She glanced across at Shannon.

"Is it true that you've discovered some cool new spells? That's what *everyone* is saying. And that you can only do them if you cover up your Sygnus with one of those." She pointed to the pink diamond on Jax's shoulder.

"No," corrected her companion. "I heard that it was something to do with Terra. Because they don't have the Sygnus there. And, like, the P stands for Portal, right?" He looked to Jax for confirmation.

"I can't tell you," responded Jax, trying not to laugh. "I'm sworn to secrecy."

"See?" said the girl to her friend. "Lucia told me that you have to figure it out for yourself, like a test or something." She turned back to Jax and blushed.

"I think it's fantastic," she said admiringly. "We're all going to wear a pink accessory to

Monday's lessons."

"Thanks," replied Jax, starting to feel a bit guilty. He exchanged a quick glance with Shannon, who was torn between laughter and horror. The rumours that Jax and Darius had started two days earlier were obviously getting a little out of control. Jax spoke again.

"You know, I'm probably not going to be wearing it for that much longer anyway, so don't worry about it too much…"

The girl tugged on the boy's arm and whispered urgently, "Let's go to Lucia's house now, and see if we can solve it today!" They backed away from Jax and Shannon, who waited until they were out of earshot before she spoke.

"That was just coincidence, right? I mean, not every underage magician we meet is going to be so gullible, surely."

But on their walk to the Seminary, they were interrupted a further three times, and each discussion followed the same lines as the first one.

Shannon shook her head in disbelief. "Who knew something like this could go viral when the internet doesn't even exist on Androva?"

"It was your idea," argued Jax. "Don't put all the blame on me! And what do you mean by going viral?"

"I'm not putting the blame on you," Shannon

replied. She felt just as bad as Jax. What had sounded fine as an idea to help Jax overcome an impossible spell seemed a bit different now that she was facing the living, breathing consequences.

"I never expected this kind of response rate," she said guiltily. "And going viral just means it's suddenly everywhere, like a contagious virus." She paused. "After what I just saw, it looks like it's Stupidity that's catching."

"Do you think I should stop wearing it?" asked Jax uncertainly.

Shannon shrugged. "Keep it on today. I might as well enjoy going out with a celebrity while it lasts," she joked. "But I want to own up to Professor Alver. It's my fault this has happened. He might be able to help us figure out a way to correct it without things getting any messier than they already are."

After dropping off the Portal Remedy to Professor Lenora, who confirmed Shannon's successful completion of the year one assessment, Jax and Shannon met up with Darius for lunch. He mentioned that he had seen Hesta that morning.

Shannon tried to keep her expression neutral, asking, "How is she?"

"Great," replied Darius. "I said you might be coming to the Seminary when your Terran school closes for summer, and she said she couldn't wait."

"Me neither," replied Shannon, attempting a smile. She intended to stick to her decision to ignore Hesta as much as possible, but she would still try to be polite.

"Is there something going on between you two?" Jax asked Darius curiously. "Hesta seems to be round here a lot lately."

Darius shook his head. "No, we're just friends."

Jax raised his eyebrows.

"No, we really are just friends!" Darius protested. "Even if I wanted to ask her out, which I *don't*, by the way, she says she's interested in someone else. She won't tell me who, but she says they're going to tell everyone soon. Apparently this other guy is trying to politely get rid of an annoying girl who won't stop hanging round him."

"Well, I'm sure it won't take long then," commented Jax. "Hesta might not be the greatest magician, but if she wants someone as her boyfriend, she usually gets them."

Shannon felt a bit sick. Hesta had obviously intended that her spiteful words would get back to Shannon. Looking at Jax, Shannon wondered, not for the first time, how he could possibly prefer her to Hesta. Then she cheered up a bit, realising that next week, Jax and Darius would be spending at least one day on Terra with her. Hesta couldn't compete with Terra. Jax and Darius were about to literally enter a whole new world.

12 Before Open Day

The twenty Council members endorsed Professor Alver and Professor Lenora's recommendation that Jax and Darius should be allowed to travel to Terra for the school Open Day. They advised minimal use of magic, with small Distraction Spells being permitted where necessary.

Jax and Darius agreed. They were happy with the idea of pretending to be Terran teenagers. On this first visit at least, they wanted to experience what life was like on Terra without magic.

Leaving the Council Assembly Chamber, Shannon thought how much things had changed for the better since her first visit. The large room was still quite intimidating, with its white stone pillars and enormous curved stone table. But the atmosphere was much more pleasant now that she was no longer seen as an enemy of Androva.

The Council ruled Androva with absolute

authority by writing and enforcing the Code, which included maintaining the list of Unauthorised Spells and appointing each magician to his or her lifetime profession at the coming of age ceremony. In contrast to Terra, where lawbreaking, uncertainty, and even terrorism were regular occurrences, Androvan life was very predictable.

When they emerged from the Council buildings, Shannon went up to Professor Alver to tell him about the pink craze they had created, and that it was getting more than a little out of control. She asked for his help in stopping it.

His mouth twitching as he tried unsuccessfully to hide a smile, the professor promised to think about it.

Shannon, Jax, and Darius spent the rest of Saturday excitedly talking about the Open Day. She would come to collect the boys through the portal at a prearranged time on Wednesday morning. Revus would close the portal afterwards, and reopen it that same evening to allow Jax and Darius to come back.

Shannon tried to prepare the boys for their visit. She realised she couldn't possibly tell them everything, so she decided to concentrate on the essentials.

"You need to be wearing something that looks like it could be a school uniform," she advised.

"Like black trousers, a white shirt, and a black sweater. And you'll have to cover your Sygnuses." Jax and Darius nodded. This wouldn't be a problem, after their recent success with the Concealing Spells.

"Will you be wearing a uniform?" asked Jax curiously.

"Yep," Shannon said. "Unfortunately I will. It's pretty hideous. I have to wear a skirt and everything."

"What's a skirt?" Jax asked, mystified. Everyone on Androva wore trousers of some kind. It didn't matter what job you did, or how old you were.

"You'll see," said Shannon. "It's like the most uncomfortable thing ever, especially invented for girls."

She explained that as far as Penny was concerned, she believed Jax and Darius lived in London.

"It will seem really weird that you don't have phones," Shannon added. "I don't exactly know what we can do about that. Maybe you can say that your headmaster is really strict and you're not allowed to use them during school hours.

"You're in year nine, like me," she added. "We'll have to invent surnames for you too."

"Surnames?" both boys repeated together, with baffled expressions.

"A surname is like your family name. No one has a Sygnus on Terra, but we have an extra name to show which family we come from."

"What's yours?" asked Jax.

"Blackwood," Shannon replied. "Actually, I have a middle name too, but no one really uses those."

"Three names?" said Darius, taken aback. "Why do you need so many?"

"Because there are a *lot* of people on Terra," Shannon said. "That will probably be the hardest thing for you to get used to. There are people, cars, and noise all day long, and sometimes all night long as well."

She had tried to explain this several times before, but she knew it would still be a shock for Jax and Darius when they first encountered it. And their lack of experience with technology would stand out because of their age.

But they had to start somewhere, and the Open Day was their best chance of learning a few things without drawing too much attention to themselves.

"Your friend Penny, she definitely doesn't know anything about Androva?" asked Darius.

"No." Shannon shook her head. "There've been a couple of times when I almost told her, but I decided it was safer for her if she didn't know. It's only recently that I've got my ability under control, remember.

"And anyway," she continued, "once you know Terra a bit better, you'll realise that keeping it secret is just easier. I don't want to find myself all over the internet as the latest freak."

A shadow passed over her face, and Jax put his arm round her, not understanding exactly what she meant, but wanting to reassure her anyway. He tried to lighten the mood.

"I don't suppose Penny likes boys with blond hair, does she?" Jax began. "Because I despair of Darius ever finding a girlfriend. Maybe if he uses a Manipulation Spell, he might stand a chance of..." Jax broke off as Darius pushed him hard in the shoulder.

"Shut up!" interrupted Darius angrily. He was very sensitive about the fact that he hadn't had a girlfriend yet. "Not all of us collect new girlfriends like new spells, you know!"

Then, realising what he had said, he turned guiltily to Shannon. "I didn't mean..." he began helplessly. "I mean, obviously things are different since Jax met you..."

Jax glared at Darius. "Thanks, Darius," he said furiously. He faced Shannon, who had stepped back from him slightly, a wary look on her face. She was thinking of what Hesta had said about Jax's dating history. Obviously there had been some truth in it.

"It doesn't matter," she said, trying to sound unconcerned. "I like you, you like me, but who knows what will happen tomorrow?"

"Darius doesn't know what he's talking about," said Jax heatedly. "He's only jealous because he likes you as well."

Shannon looked at Darius in surprise. Darius opened his mouth to deny what Jax had said, but then closed it again. It was true that he thought Shannon was amazing. But he had always known nothing would come of it after seeing how she felt about Jax. And now he was happy just to be her friend.

There was a pause as the three underage magicians tried to deal with these conversational bombshells. No one wanted to speak first, in case they made things worse.

Finally, Shannon couldn't bear the silence any longer. "As it happens," she said to Darius, "Penny isn't seeing anyone, so why don't you make friends with her and see how it goes?"

Darius, relieved, tried to keep the conversation going. "What's she like?" he asked.

"She's amazing," Shannon replied, her face relaxing as she thought about her best friend. "Really loyal and funny, but kind of crazy too. She's always trying out new make-up and hairstyles, so even by Terran standards, she's got quite a unique look."

"I can't wait to meet her," said Darius truthfully. "And what will we do once the Open Day is finished? Just hang out?"

"I thought we could go to the cinema," Shannon said enthusiastically. "There's a new superhero film showing, and it's the closest thing you'll see to real-life magic. It's obviously not real, but it's a pretty convincing copy of it."

The conversation continued more easily after that, and eventually they were all able to pretend that the previous discussion hadn't happened. When Jax took Shannon down to the portal room that evening, he waited for a moment before he activated the symbols.

"Look," he began, pulling her towards him, his green eyes serious. "I really like you," he continued. "More than I've ever liked anyone."

Shannon gave a slight shrug. "I like you too," she replied in a small voice.

"Then we're OK?" he asked. Shannon nodded. Holding her face gently between his hands, he gave her a kiss. When he took his hands away, Shannon could see that they were faintly glowing, and she could feel the buzz against her skin.

"See you on Wednesday," he said, stepping back to open the portal.

"Wednesday," she agreed, turning to walk through it.

The next three days crawled by on Terra. Shannon and Penny went to a meeting at their school to learn what they were supposed to do during the Open Day.

They had to make sure that the prospective new students saw all the facilities, and that they attended a couple of lessons as well. There was going to be a basketball tournament during the afternoon in the indoor sports hall. There would also be displays of project work in some of the classrooms.

Penny was driving Shannon slowly mad with her endless questions about Jax and Darius. On top of that, she had received a call from Toni Maxwell, who wanted to set a date for Shannon to visit the InterPharm laboratory and offices. They agreed on the first week of the summer holidays, Shannon thinking that she might as well get it out of the way.

Penny was very keen for Shannon to bring back the promised make-up samples. Decora, InterPharm's luxury cosmetics brand, was far too expensive for the girls to buy for themselves, and Penny couldn't wait to try it.

At least there was no more homework being set, so Shannon was able to learn some new spells instead. This made the evenings go much faster than the long, slow days.

She had borrowed a book on elementary

Manipulation Spells from Jax, knowing that there were more spells in this particular discipline than any other. She wanted to get a head start so that she didn't disappoint Professor Alver when she started at the Seminary.

It was actually good fun playing around with shapes, colours, and textures. The first evening she made her carpet grow tall and thick, like indoor grass. The next evening, she messed around with some of her clothes, changing the colours.

She was delighted to realise that she could lengthen her favourite skinny jeans, which she had been on the verge of growing out of.

She returned Boris the Bear to his normal size. And keeping Tammy out of her room was easy now. She just had to increase the size of her bedroom door very slightly. Then it would be stuck in the doorframe, unable to be opened until she reduced it again.

Finally, Wednesday morning arrived. Shannon received three texts from Penny before she had even got dressed.

"**What r u wearing???**"

"**This is going to be awesome!!**"

"**Text me when you get there!!!!**"

Shannon had said that she couldn't walk to school with Penny because she was going to meet Jax and Darius at the station off the London train. Fortunately, the station wasn't too far away from their school, so this was a believable explanation. She couldn't exactly let Penny see her and the boys arriving in the woods out of thin air.

Nervously, Shannon checked her appearance in the mirror. She was wearing her usual uniform of knee-length skirt, black tights, and flat shoes.

Her white shirt was half tucked in, and the school tie in grey and green stripes was loosely tied around the shirt collar. She had left her hair down, having used straighteners on it that morning, and was wearing mascara and lip gloss.

She didn't usually wear make-up when she went to Androva, because no one else seemed to. But she couldn't go barefaced to school. Her friends would notice and ask her about it. She hoped Jax wouldn't think it looked too weird.

She found that she couldn't eat any breakfast, and left the house early, reassuring her mother that she was just excited about representing the school at the Open Day. After quickly checking that the street was quiet, she entered the woods and made her way to the portal location.

Right on time, she saw the shimmer, and she stepped through it. She knew Revus would not let the boys walk through until Shannon had confirmed that the coast was clear on the other side.

For a moment, Shannon stood there on the spellstation while Jax and Darius looked her up and down. "What?" she said apprehensively. "What is it?"

"You look…" Jax swallowed. He was slightly taken aback by the sight of Shannon. She looks amazing, he thought. Suddenly he felt embarrassed about the reassuring words he had said on Saturday. Looking as she did, it seemed more likely that Shannon would get bored of him, rather than the other way around.

"You look nearly rice. I mean really nice!" he corrected himself hastily, a bit flustered. Revus turned away to hide a smile at the sight of his fourteen-year-old son losing his cool for once.

Shannon tried to look laid-back about it, but was secretly very pleased.

"Are you ready?" she asked them.

She stepped backwards onto Terran soil, and Jax and Darius followed her.

13 Distraction Spell Number One

Shannon led the way through the woods back to her street, feeling a bit shy now that Jax and Darius were actually here.

"Wait." Jax stopped her, tugging on her hand. "Please can we stop for a minute?"

"Yes," agreed Darius, "I have to stop too."

Shannon turned round to look at them, and immediately realised what the problem was. Both boys were glowing slightly, and she could feel the buzz of energy from the surrounding trees reaching out to them.

"There's so much living magic," whispered Darius. "I'd forgotten what it's like here."

Jax looked at Shannon curiously. "How do you hide it?" he asked her. "I know your force field is at least as strong as mine, if not stronger. But looking at you now, I wouldn't even know it was there."

Shannon looked unhappy for a moment. "It's

not easy. Most of the time I have half a headache because I have to suppress it so much. But what choice do I have? If I don't hide it, then I'll only have to deal with a load of other problems.

"Anyway," she continued, "it's much more difficult just here. These woods have been around for hundreds of years. They're like one giant force field all on their own. Once we get into the town, there's almost nothing green, and you'll hardly notice any living magic at all."

She waited as Jax and Darius concentrated on suppressing their magic so that it receded out of sight. Then she remembered something.

"Don't move," she instructed, getting out her phone. She quickly took several pictures of them both.

"Finally!" she said, smiling. "Now I'll be able to see your ugly faces whenever I want to," she added jokingly.

"Show me!" Jax demanded, grabbing the phone. He quickly figured out how to swipe between the photos, looking at them in disbelief.

He turned the phone over in his hands, unable to understand how the small device could create such a perfect miniature reproduction. He held the phone out to Darius, who widened his eyes in shock when he saw the photos.

"That's impossible…" Darius said.

Shannon grinned at their reaction. "You don't

know the half of it," she promised. Then, worried they were going to be late, she suggested they start walking.

Shannon couldn't help glancing up at the neighbour's house as they passed it, sure she could see the man watching again.

As Shannon had known they would be, Jax and Darius were shocked when they saw their first car speeding past. The closer they got to the school, the busier the roads became.

"How do they not hit each other?" asked Darius. "And how do you know they're not going to hit *us*?"

"Sometimes they do," replied Shannon, and then noticing Darius's look of horror, she added, "but don't worry, there *are* rules about how the whole driving thing works."

"What's it like, being in a car?" asked Jax, stepping back from the edge of the pavement slightly. "I mean, travelling so fast and everything."

"I suppose I don't really notice it anymore," said Shannon. "It doesn't feel so fast when you're on the inside." Seeing that Jax looked a bit disappointed to hear this, she had a thought.

"I know what we can do another time, though, if you want to go fast. We can go on a rollercoaster! They're pretty cool."

"A rollercoaster?" Jax repeated the strange

sounding word.

Shannon got out her phone to text Penny.

"**5 mins away**," she typed.

"**Awesome!!!**" came the immediate reply.

Jax and Darius were looking eagerly over her shoulder.

"That was a text message?" Jax asked.

"Yes," Shannon confirmed.

"It really is like talking," said Darius. "It's so fast. How close does the other person have to be?"

"They can be anywhere," replied Shannon.

"Anywhere?" said Darius. "Anywhere in the same city, or…?"

"Anywhere on Terra, pretty much," confirmed Shannon. Darius looked at Jax in amazement.

Then he took the phone off Shannon, typing rather laboriously, "**Hello Penny, this is Darius**."

He looked up at Shannon, saying, "Can I send her a photo?"

"You catch on fast!" said Shannon, a bit surprised. She showed Darius how to take a selfie, then added it to the text message.

There was a short delay after Darius pressed Send.

Then "**OMG Shannon Blackwood!**" came the reply. "**u had better not be winding me up!!**"

"What does that mean?" asked a confused Darius.

"Don't worry, it's good," answered Shannon with a grin, typing "**c u in 5**" before putting her phone away.

Jax looked at Darius, feeling a bit taken aback. It seemed like Darius was finding this easier than he was.

There were more and more people on the pavement the closer they got to the school. Jax and Darius were starting to wonder how Shannon would possibly be able to find her friend, when someone ran up to them.

"Hey!" greeted Penny, slightly breathless, and Shannon gave her an answering smile.

"This is Jax, and this is Darius," Shannon said, introducing the two boys. Penny looked at them for a moment, registering that not only were both boys totally gorgeous, but that they had a kind of aura, almost as if they were celebrities or something.

Penny turned back to Shannon. Her eyes were huge, and she seemed incapable of speech.

"What?" asked Shannon innocently. Penny lost for words was not something that happened very often, and she was going to make the most of it.

"I... you..." Penny tried.

"It's great to finally meet you, Penny," said

Darius, feeling sorry for her. She smiled at him gratefully, and he noticed that her blue eyes, emphasised by layers of iridescent green eyeshadow, were very pretty.

As the four teenagers went into the school to find the Open Day registration desk, Penny and Darius walked together behind Jax and Shannon.

Hesitantly, and then with more confidence, they started talking. Penny's naturally engaging personality gradually resurfaced, and Darius laughed a couple of times at her descriptions of school life.

Jax leaned in to Shannon, saying in a low voice, "She's nice." Then he asked, "Are we doing OK? Do you think anyone realises?"

Shannon smothered a laugh. "No, you'll pass for ordinary teenagers so far," she whispered. "I think we'd know about it if anyone realised you were actually aliens in disguise."

After registration, where Jax's and Darius's made-up surnames and London school were accepted without comment, they started their tour of the school.

The boys found that despite the large size of the school grounds, and the many separate buildings, everything felt quite closed in and cluttered compared to the Seminary.

"There's not much space," murmured Jax to Shannon. "You couldn't do many spells in these rooms."

"Well, duh!" responded Shannon with a smile. "Just as well there *aren't* any spells then, isn't it?"

Darius and Penny had stopped to peer into one of the classrooms in the Humanities block. They all went in to look at some Year Eight history project work on Henry VIII.

Jax and Darius at first thought it was fiction, and were incredulous when Shannon assured them it had all really happened.

"Good job this Terran didn't have magic at his disposal too!" said Jax to Shannon in a low voice.

"Can we go into an actual lesson?" asked Darius.

"What's the point?" replied Jax dismissively. "Everything's going to be done with words and books. It'll be boring."

Shannon felt herself becoming a bit annoyed on behalf of her school. "It's not always boring," she protested.

Penny looked at her. "Isn't it?" she asked, in genuine surprise. Jax and Darius laughed, and Shannon gave a reluctant smile.

"As it happens," she began, "we *are* supposed to take you into a lesson as part of the Open Day. So... how about ICT? We'll have to be quick though, I think the bell's about to ring."

As if to prove her right, the bell rang that very moment, and children started appearing in the corridor from the classrooms around them.

Penny agreed with Shannon. "She's right, we have to go. Otherwise we'll just get a lecture from Mr. Andrews. And too much of my short life has already been wasted on those," she added grumpily.

"Anyway, ICT this close to the end of term will be cool. They'll probably be playing games."

"ICT," repeated Darius, trying to sound as if he knew what that meant. "Yeah, OK."

Shannon led the way out of the Humanities block and across to ICT.

"What is ICT?" whispered Jax to Shannon as they walked.

"You'll like it, I promise." She smiled. "It's I for Information, C for Communication, and the T stands for Technologies…"

Jax looked pleased. Terran technology was what he had been looking forward to the most. So far, he was finding this school very disorienting. With his magic force field suppressed so severely, he felt off balance. As if he were constantly on the verge of dizziness or something.

And knowing that he couldn't easily use magic to get himself out of trouble made him anxious, an emotion he was completely unaccustomed to feeling.

They arrived at the ICT room at the same time

as the teacher, Miss Stevens. "Ah, Shannon, Penny," she said briskly, "I saw your names on the Open Day register. Well done. And who do you have with you today?"

"Jax and Darius," offered Penny. "They're from London," she added.

"Indeed?" said Miss Stevens, turning to the boys as she shifted the folders she was holding into a more comfortable position.

"Year Nine as well?" They nodded uncertainly. "Then perhaps you might share with us what you've been learning in ICT this term? I'm sure it would help my students to get a different perspective."

Jax and Darius looked at Shannon for help.

"They don't really do ICT at their school," said Shannon quickly, before immediately realising that sounded ridiculous. Penny and Miss Stevens both looked at her in bewilderment.

"But it's on the National Curriculum," said Miss Stevens.

"Um, their school is more of an international school," replied Shannon. "Their lessons don't follow the usual subjects."

"What?" asked Penny, her brow furrowed in confusion. "Do you come from a different country then?" she asked Darius.

Shannon was starting to panic. The more she tried not to tell an actual lie, the more implausible her explanations sounded. She saw Jax step behind Miss Stevens and Penny. "Keep talking," he said with a mischievous grin. "You're explaining it so much better than I could."

Penny and Miss Stevens glanced at Jax for a second, before turning back to Shannon expectantly. "Um…" she tried again. "It's hard to describe, their school doesn't really use technology in the same way that we do…"

Then she realised what Jax was going to do, and sighed with relief. He closed his eyes for a second, releasing a small amount of magic to create a Distraction Spell. Darius looked up and down the corridor to check that the five of them were alone.

"Well, I've never heard anything so…" Miss Stevens began. She turned to look at Jax, and he gave her an innocent smile. Then he reached out to pat both Penny and Miss Stevens on the arm. He didn't want to actually project the spell, in case someone saw them.

Immediately, Miss Stevens pushed past them to enter the classroom. "Come along, don't stand out in the corridor all day!" she called, looking behind her briefly. Shannon was relieved to see that the Distraction Spell had worked as quickly as usual.

Penny blinked a couple of times. She looked down at Jax's hands, which were by his sides again. He opened them up, as if to show her that they were empty, and gave her an enquiring look.

"What was I saying?" asked Penny with a frown.

"Nothing important," said Shannon, turning to go into the classroom and hoping that Penny would follow her.

Because the class was only half full, they managed to find seats at the back. Shannon was glad, as she didn't want anyone else to see Jax's and Darius's screens while they were learning.

They attracted a few curious looks, and Naomi, Penny and Shannon's friend, realised that one of the boys must be Shannon's famous secret boyfriend. She had just leaned back in her seat to demand an introduction, when Miss Stevens clapped her hands.

"Settle down!" she said, raising her voice to get everyone's attention. "I've got an entertaining assignment for you this morning."

A couple of people groaned. "Aren't we supposed to be playing games, Miss Stevens?" asked someone near the front.

"Not this morning," replied the teacher. "But thank you for your enthusiasm."

She went on to describe the assignment. In groups of four, using only a tablet computer, they would have to create a short video report discussing the possibility of life on other planets.

The finished film needed to be less than one minute long, and would have to show a view that either supported the possibility or contested it.

"There are seventeen of you in class today, so one group will have to be made up of five," said Miss Stevens. "We will watch your films at the end of the lesson. You only have forty-five minutes, so I suggest you get started."

Chattering immediately broke out as everyone split up into their various teams, leaving Shannon, Penny, Jax, and Darius to form a group at the back.

Shannon looked at Jax, then Darius. "Fascinating subject!" she said, half laughing.

Penny scoffed. "Obviously there's no life on other planets!" she said, looking at the others expectantly. "That's what our report should say, don't you all agree?"

14 Aliens Walk Amongst Us

Shannon swallowed. This was going to be interesting. Jax leaned forward. "How do you know there's no life on other planets?" he asked Penny.

"Because no one's ever proved it?" she responded, folding her arms defensively.

"What if I told you that *I* came from another planet?" he said seriously.

Penny laughed, assuming Jax was joking, then hesitated for a moment as his face remained completely unsmiling. "You're not…" she said, slightly uncertainly.

"Are you absolutely convinced about that?" Jax said. "You look like you might not be totally sure." He deliberately allowed his magic force field to expand a bit. Not enough to be visible, but enough so that Penny, sitting next to him, could feel goosebumps starting to form on her arm.

"OK, I am officially getting freaked out," she said, turning to Shannon for support. Shannon frowned at Jax before she answered, noticing a glimmer of amusement in his green eyes.

"Jax is just messing with you," Shannon said. "*Aren't* you, Jax?"

Jax shrugged, suppressing his magic again.

"But it's an interesting idea for our video," Shannon continued. "Why don't we just film Jax and Darius pretending to be from another planet? Let's see if we can make someone else in the class believe it too."

"Film us?" queried Jax. "You mean like a moving photo with one of your technology devices?"

Penny's eyes widened.

"Yeah," replied Shannon, "and it's good to see that you're getting into character already. Nice use of alien vocab."

She turned to Penny. "What do you think? If even half the class is as easy to fool as you, it might work."

Penny made a face. "I'm not easy to fool!"

Shannon looked at her sceptically. "You are. You totally believed that Jax was an alien just then."

"I didn't!" Penny argued. "I just don't know him very well, and I went along with it so that I didn't hurt his feelings." She looked sideways at

Darius for a second, and he smiled at her reassuringly. Even though they were best friends, sometimes Darius felt like using his strongest Containment Spell on Jax to prevent him from being such an idiot. This was one of those occasions.

"But I do think it's a good idea for the assignment," Penny added. "Can I be the interviewer?"

Shannon nodded. She hated being filmed, so that was fine with her. They sat both boys next to each other, and after a quick discussion on the list of questions, started recording.

Shannon suggested that the boys should just make up their answers rather than read from a script, to try to make it sound more convincing. Of course, she knew that there was no need for prepared answers. They could just tell the truth.

Two of the other groups were searching the internet for pictures and video clips about other planets, and one was doing a mock interview like Penny with a pretend expert on alien life. Shannon noticed her phone buzzing with a text, and saw that Naomi had asked her, "**Which one is Jax?**"

She looked across the room at Naomi to catch her eye. Then she nodded towards Jax, who was speaking into the tablet's camera in response to one of Penny's questions. Naomi gave her a thumbs up and a big grin.

After the interview was finished, they started to edit it. Jax and Darius were fascinated with the way they looked and sounded on the screen.

They kept replaying the same bits over and over, until Shannon told them sharply to get a grip.

"Don't worry," Penny told her, unconcerned. "All guys are secretly in love with watching themselves, there's nothing we can do about it."

Shannon laughed at the boys' expressions when they heard this.

Finally, with five minutes to spare, they had a final version of their report. Naomi wandered over to be introduced to Jax and Darius, followed by Patrick, who wanted to make sure the newcomers realised Naomi already had a boyfriend.

Miss Stevens asked everyone to bring their tablets to the front of the classroom, and then she played the films one at a time on the large screen.

The interview of Jax and Darius was shown last. Penny played the part of the sceptical reporter, asking the boys to explain why the audience should believe that they were from another planet.

At first, the other teenagers in the classroom laughed when Penny put this question to the two boys.

"We know your planet as Terra," began Darius. "This is our first proper visit during daylight, though we have been here many times under cover of darkness."

"You might be able to tell that there is something different about us. We will do our best to hide it, but it is there nonetheless," added Jax, direct to camera.

"Once you were more like us than you know," continued Darius. "But now you have forgotten everything."

"We are not here to force you to remember," said Jax. He gave a small smile, which looked quite unfriendly, as the expression in his eyes remained completely cold.

"But I cannot promise that you won't remember all the same. Or that you will like it when you do."

There was silence as the interview finished.

"Well…" began Miss Stevens nervously. "That was an interesting angle." Getting up to switch off the screen, she recovered herself.

"You boys have the makings of very good actors! I'm sure we all appreciate you coming to the Open Day and taking part in our class today."

The bell rang for lunchtime, and the class began to break up. Some of the others looked at Jax and Darius a bit warily, and Shannon smiled inwardly. It was weird how some people seemed to sense that Jax and Darius were different, but others ignored it.

Penny had definitely been a bit dazed when she first met them, but Mr. Andrews at the registration desk had seemed completely oblivious. Perhaps it was an age thing.

The group of four headed to the cafeteria and joined the line for pizza and chips. Shannon offered to buy Darius and Jax some chocolate, knowing how much they had liked it the last time.

They found a table and were soon joined by Naomi, Patrick, Megan, Leo, and Freddy, who had finally asked Megan out the previous week.

"That was a cool film you made about the whole 'aliens are walking amongst us' thing," Patrick started. Jax smiled.

"Did you believe it?" he asked curiously.

"Well, there's this website…" Patrick continued, and everyone gave their usual groan.

"Patrick likes to search out the dregs of the internet and present them to us as true facts," explained Shannon.

"I'll send you the link," offered Patrick. "What's your number?"

"I don't have a phone," replied Jax, feeling disappointed. He was starting to realise that being a teenager on Terra without a phone was a little bit like being a teenager on Androva with no magical ability.

"He doesn't have his phone *with* him," corrected Shannon.

"Well he can still give me the number, can't he?" said Patrick reasonably.

Shannon hesitated. "Well, he's between contracts, aren't you?" she said, turning to Jax, who shrugged. He had no idea if what Shannon was saying made sense. "So his number might be changing."

Patrick rolled his eyes and handed his phone over to Jax so that he could look at the website.

"A word of advice, mate," he said in a low voice, "don't let her do *all* the talking for you. I know from experience that's a bad road to go down."

Jax laughed. Shannon and Naomi, who had heard Patrick despite his low voice, both scowled.

Lunchtime passed quickly, with Jax and Darius surprised at how much they enjoyed themselves. The food wasn't great, but they found the fizzy drinks amusing, and the chocolate tasted as good as they both remembered.

They noticed that teenagers on Terra were much less concerned with the rules than underage magicians were on Androva. Performing well at school also seemed to be something that no one was particularly worried about.

On Androva, everyone knew that their performance at the Seminary would determine the profession assigned to them by the Council when they came of age. No one wanted to be stuck in a job they hated.

But on Terra, it was as if the students didn't care about any of that. Most of them just wanted to have fun. Jax and Darius found it very appealing.

There was a lot of talk of the summer holidays, and making plans for meeting up. Shannon's suggestion of going to the local amusement park was greeted with enthusiasm.

"Rollercoasters," she whispered to Jax.

He raised his eyebrows. "An *amusement* park? You mean, the only purpose in going there is to have fun?" he replied incredulously.

"Yep." She nodded.

Patrick and Leo were also determined to reach the final level of a computer game they were both playing. They were obviously very competitive about who would get there first. Jax and Darius had to admit that they hadn't played it.

Jax painted a picture of a very strict school and very strict parents. He said that this was why he and Darius were looking to change schools, even though it would mean a longer journey.

Patrick tried to explain the game to Jax, and

showed him the trailer for it on his phone. Jax was intrigued.

The chance to play at being someone else, and go on a dangerous mission without actually getting hurt for real, was quite attractive. Like being in a training room, but much more sophisticated. And you could actually stop and go back to it as many times as you wanted.

These Terrans don't need to discover other worlds, he thought. They can enter different realities any time they want to, using their books and their technology.

After lunch Shannon and Penny took Jax and Darius to the sports hall to watch the basketball competition. Freddy went with them, as he was playing in the first game, but everyone else had to go back to lessons.

Jax and Darius continued to be the object of some puzzled glances. They weren't doing too badly at suppressing their force fields, but occasionally, if they were distracted, they forgot for a moment.

They weren't projecting spells or anything, so there was no magic actually visible, but a few people still noticed something different.

As they sat down to watch the game, Darius told Penny that basketball was not one of the sports allowed by their school, so she explained the rules to him and Jax. Both teams were evenly matched, and by the fourth quarter there were only three points between them.

Jax and Darius were riveted. They cheered just as loudly as everyone else when Freddy finally broke through the opposing team's defence and scored a particularly impressive shot to clinch the game.

"That was amazing!" said Jax, turning to Shannon. "Are all Terran sports this much fun? Can I try it?"

Shannon glanced at Penny, worried that she'd heard Jax use the word "Terran," but fortunately Penny was in the middle of telling Darius about the school's performance in the regional basketball league that term.

"We could go to one of the outside courts," said Shannon, considering. "Two of them are used for tennis at this time of year, but I think there's one that still has the basketball hoops up."

"Tennis? What's that?" asked Jax. Penny, catching this, turned round and gave him a curious look.

"I mean, I am an alien," said Jax hastily, "I can't be expected to know these things."

Penny laughed, and Shannon gave Jax warning look. He tried to look apologetic, but he was finding it increasingly difficult to speak so carefully all the time.

It was easier for Shannon, he thought.

Everyone on Androva knew she was from a different world, so she didn't have to pretend. Now that he had seen a bit more of Terra, he wanted to ask a thousand questions. But he would have to wait until he and Shannon were alone again before he could even start.

"Do you want to try shooting some hoops then?" asked Shannon.

"I do!" answered Darius.

"Yeah, that would be cool," agreed Jax. "Let's do it."

15 Distraction Spell Number Two

Five minutes later, they were back outside. Shannon thought they should probably tour all the sports facilities on their way, so as to keep up the Open Day pretence.

"Football, Hockey, Cricket, Netball, Athletics," she recited as they walked, "oh, and obviously Tennis," she added with a grin.

Jax and Darius tried to nod as if they knew what she was talking about. Shannon had picked up a couple of basketballs from the PE cupboard, and Jax and Darius were bouncing them experimentally as they walked along.

When they arrived at the row of outside courts, Shannon was glad to see that the far court did still have its hoops. The boys wasted no time in trying some practice shots, finding it surprisingly difficult to send the ball accurately to its target. It had looked so simple during the match they had just watched.

"It would be so much easier if..." Jax muttered to Darius.

"No, Jax," replied Darius in a low voice. "Using magic would be cheating. Not to mention dangerous as well."

"Yes, but using magic is what we *do*," Jax argued. "Who are we if we're not magicians?"

"We're not magicians today," said Darius firmly.

"Get on with it!" shouted Penny from the edge of the court. "Or do you want me and Shannon to come and show you how it's done?"

"You play?" asked Darius.

"Better than you!" responded Penny with a cheeky grin. She walked towards them, rolling up the sleeves of her shirt as she did so. As she got close to Darius, he backed away, bouncing the basketball by his side.

Easily, she took possession of the ball, bounced it a few steps, and then threw it to Shannon, who made a perfect shot into the hoop at her end of the court.

"Aliens can't play basketball apparently!" called Shannon. Jax and Darius rose to the challenge. As they practiced a bit more, they started to improve, until eventually they were scoring as often as the girls. Everyone was disappointed when the bell rang for the end of school. But Shannon reminded Jax and Darius that they were going to the cinema, and they cheered up immediately.

"Is Penny coming with us?" asked Darius. "I mean, if she wants to, of course," he added hastily.

"I'd love to," said Penny quickly. "I mean, if you want me to, of course."

Shannon grinned. "What about what Jax and I want? Can we check that too?" she teased.

"Ha, ha, very funny," responded Penny, trying not to look embarrassed.

The cinema trip was a great success. Jax and Darius were genuinely amazed by the experience. Though Shannon had warned them that most of what they would see was special effects and not real, they soon forgot this and became totally immersed in the story.

Jax held Shannon's hand, and to her amusement, his grip definitely tightened during the scary parts. As they emerged into the early evening sunshine afterwards, both boys looked a bit dazed while they struggled to get their minds back to reality.

"Now what?" asked Penny. "Do you guys have to get the train or something?"

She was disappointed that Darius hadn't asked for her mobile number yet. She wondered if she should ask for his number instead. Darius, on the other hand, knew enough about Terra by now to realise that his not having a mobile was going to be a problem. He liked Penny, and definitely wanted to stay in contact with her. But how could he do it?

"My phone is broken," he said suddenly. "Otherwise I would get your number…"

"Oh," said Penny in relief. "Well, do you have an email address or something?"

Darius looked at Shannon. "Er…"

"Both our parents are so strict about all that," said Jax. "They like to think they live on a world where email doesn't exist or something," he added truthfully.

"Oh," said Penny again, disappointed.

"But I'll come back, during the summer holidays," said Darius, taking hold of her hand. "I promise. And I'll try to figure something out about the phone." He looked into her eyes earnestly, and Penny decided to believe him.

"Anyway, let's go and get a sandwich at my house," suggested Shannon. "We still have an hour or so before we have to be at the port… at the station," she corrected herself hurriedly.

"I don't know why I said port—it's not like you're going back by boat," she said, making a feeble joke.

They were just finishing their sandwiches when Shannon's mother arrived home with Tammy. Shannon introduced Jax and Darius, saying that she and Penny had met them during the Open Day.

Mrs. Blackwood was welcoming, but obviously a bit tired and distracted, which Shannon saw as a good thing. Jax and Darius were getting tired as well, and being so close to the garden and the woodland was making it more and more of a challenge to keep their force fields hidden.

Tammy was looking at Jax curiously. He gave her an enquiring look in return, not sure how to behave. He had no brothers or sisters of his own, and neither did Darius. Large families were rare on Androva.

"Time to get ready for bed, Tammy," said Shannon's mother. Tammy pointed at Jax.

"I've seen you before," she announced.

"What?" said Shannon and her mother at the same time.

"You were in my dream once," continued Tammy. "Collecting fairy dust from the garden."

Jax couldn't prevent a look of panic from crossing his face as he exchanged a glance with Shannon. Mrs. Blackwood had already dismissed Tammy's words, however, and was pulling her younger daughter by the hand to take her upstairs.

"Not more tales of fairy dust," she said tiredly. "We're going to have to have a serious word with you about all this magic talk, young lady."

Penny started laughing, which fortunately broke the tension and allowed Shannon to pretend to laugh as well.

"Your sister is priceless, Shannon," said Penny. "Wasn't she going on about magic the other weekend too? I wish I was still young enough to believe in all that stuff."

"Can we leave now?" asked Jax abruptly. He was feeling quite uneasy all of a sudden, and wanted to speak to Shannon in private.

Shannon made a big show of noticing the time, and said she would have to call a taxi for Jax and Darius to get to the station on time.

Penny, who had been hoping to walk to the station with them, was further disappointed when Shannon said there was no need for Penny to wait for the taxi.

Shannon said she was exhausted and wanted to get an early night. Reluctantly Penny left to walk home, after whispering to Shannon, "You'd better text me later!"

Darius gave Penny a quick hug as he said goodbye, which cheered her up a bit.

"What just happened?" asked Jax urgently as soon as Penny had left. He kept his voice low so that Shannon's mother would not hear. "Did your sister really just say that?"

"I don't know," responded Shannon. "I've never heard her mention it before. She saw me do a Reduction Spell a couple of weeks ago—"

"*What?*" said Jax, interrupting her, his voice rising.

"I meant to tell you, but then I was late for the dinner, and then we were working on the Concealing Spell, and it just never seemed the right time," Shannon said helplessly.

"Let's not overreact here," said Darius. "She's only a child, and it doesn't look like anyone is going to believe her."

"Can she keep a secret?" asked Jax.

Shannon bit her lip. Then she shook her head.

"It's too soon," said Jax resolutely. "It's too soon for anyone to know about Androva."

He paced up and down as he spoke.

"We have to find out more about Terra before we can let anyone know about us. I should have realised this before, but it's dangerous here. All this time I've believed that Androva had nothing to fear, because we have magic."

He stopped pacing to look at Shannon, before adding, "I was wrong."

Shannon opened her mouth to say something in defence of Terra, but then realised there was nothing she could say.

"That King Henry guy, he really did those things?" Jax checked. Shannon nodded. "And the bad guys in the film we just saw, and the pretend war in that computer game Patrick had? Guns, fighting, evil people, that's not just in fiction, is it?"

Shannon shook her head unhappily.

"I don't know if magic can stop a bullet," said Jax, "but I'd like to find out before someone tries to shoot me."

Darius was watching Jax with a small smile. "What is it?" Jax asked him. "Don't you agree with me?"

"I do agree with you," Darius said. "When you put it like that, how could I not?"

"Then why are you smiling?" Jax challenged him.

"Don't take this the wrong way, but I just think that if your father were here, he would be very proud of you," replied Darius.

Jax paused for a moment while he considered this, and then he gave Darius a very small smile in return.

"What should we do?" asked Shannon. "I feel really bad about this. I never meant for Tammy to see me, it was an accident."

Jax put his hand on her arm to reassure her. "No one's blaming you. I've taken some crazy risks myself, after all. But we have to stop your sister from telling anyone else. For her own protection as well as Androva's."

He looked at Darius. "Distraction Spell by recall?" he suggested. Darius nodded, while

Shannon looked mystified. Jax turned back to her to explain.

"Normally Distraction Spells only work in the moment—when you're distracting someone from what's actually happening. But if you can get the person to recall something that happened in the past, and then use the Distraction Spell while they are thinking about it... then they will usually forget."

Shannon was contemplating this when her mother reappeared.

"Has Penny gone?" she asked, looking round.

"Yes," replied Shannon. "We're just about to leave ourselves. I'm going to walk part of the way back to the station with Jax and Darius."

"Well, make sure you're back home before it's dark," warned her mother. "And keep your phone with you."

Shannon nodded. "I will." Then she saw Jax raising his eyebrows at her expectantly. "Actually, Mum," continued Shannon, "can I bring Tammy down quickly to say goodnight to Jax and Darius?"

"I suppose so," said her mother, "though please don't encourage this fantasy she has about seeing fairy dust and magic everywhere. She wouldn't stop going on about it upstairs just now."

Shannon exchanged a glance with Jax and

Darius. If they had had any doubts about doing the spell, they were now completely gone.

Tammy came down holding her sister's hand and wearing pyjamas with ponies on them. She looked at Jax and Darius shyly, holding her elephant toy under one arm.

Shannon led her over to Jax and Darius, and Jax bent down to talk to her. Darius edged sideways slightly, until he was standing next to Mrs. Blackwood.

"Tammy, you know what you said earlier about seeing me in one of your dreams?" began Jax. "And you know when you thought you saw your big sister using magic too?"

Tammy nodded, her eyes wide.

"Can you remember them clearly?" continued Jax. "Can you see them inside your head?"

Tammy nodded again, this time more fiercely.

Jax kept his hands clasped together in front of him, but Shannon could see the spell starting to form.

Shannon's mother clicked her tongue exasperatedly. "Please can we *not* talk about this…"

Her voice trailed off as Darius touched her arm. At the same time, Jax gently patted Tammy's elbow. Immediately both boys stepped back, and Shannon looked nervously at her mother and her sister. Please work, she said to herself. Please, please work.

16 A Question Of Trust

"Don't forget to take your phone with you, Shannon," Mrs. Blackwood said, then hesitated. "Or did I already say that?"

"Yes, Mum," said Shannon, "you did, and I won't forget."

Tammy yawned. "I'm tired," she said. Then she looked up at Jax and smiled a bit cheekily. "Are you Shannon's boyfriend?" she asked.

Shannon's mother laughed. "Don't embarrass your sister, Tammy. Come on, let's get you to bed."

"Nice to meet you, Tammy," said Jax as she let her mother lead her back upstairs.

"Thank you for the hospitality," added Darius politely to Mrs. Blackwood.

"You're very welcome," she replied with a smile. "I hope we'll see you both again?" she added, turning to include Jax.

"I hope so too," replied Darius.

Shannon, Jax, and Darius then left the house, waiting until they were some way into the woods before heaving huge sighs of relief.

"Will it definitely be OK?" asked Shannon. "I mean, doing a spell on someone as young as Tammy?"

"Yes," replied Jax firmly. "It makes no difference."

Shannon was reassured. Checking the time, she realised they still had a little while before the portal would open. The sky was darkening in advance of sunset, and the woods were deserted.

"It's so quiet," commented Darius. "All day long, it's been so noisy here. But now it's finally quiet again."

"This has felt like the longest day of my life," added Jax.

"Really?" asked Shannon. "What about when you were interrogated?"

Jax allowed himself a wry smile. "That was the longest *night* of my life," he clarified.

The deeper they walked into the woods, the more the buzz of living magic reached out to them. Jax and Darius were glowing again.

Shannon was finding it difficult to keep her own force field suppressed after such a tiring day, so it was hardly surprising that Jax and Darius were losing the battle to keep theirs under control.

They were silent for a few moments as they waited. Then Jax spoke.

"Saturday morning, usual time?" he asked. Shannon agreed. She still had two more days of school left before term ended, and she thought that a couple of days of normality before returning to Androva would not be a bad thing.

"What shall I tell Penny though?" she asked, turning to Darius.

"Tell her I'm looking forward to seeing her again," replied Darius.

"Did you like her then?" asked Shannon, wanting to be sure before she got Penny's hopes up.

"Yes," replied Darius, going very slightly pink as Shannon grinned at him.

"I'm glad," Shannon said. "I can tell that she likes you too."

"And in the meantime I'm going to give some serious thought to how I can get Terran technology to work on Androva," continued Darius. "It's something we need to figure out anyway, if we're going to learn how to protect ourselves from it."

Jax had remained silent during this exchange, his expression thoughtful. Darius looked across at him.

"You'll help me, won't you? Wouldn't it be so much easier if you could contact Shannon using technology, without having to wait for the next portal time?"

"I don't know…" said Jax. "I mean, yes, it would be easier, and yes, I would love to talk to Shannon more often. I don't know about you and Penny though…"

"What do you mean?" asked Darius, confused.

"I'm not sure it's safe to get close to a Terran until we've figured a few things out. The risk of her finding out about us is much greater if you're friends with her. We don't want to be using Distraction Spells every five minutes."

"But what about you and Shannon?" said Darius, feeling a bit angry at the way Jax was making decisions on his behalf. "*She's* a Terran as well!"

"Well, she is, but she's a magician too," argued Jax reasonably. "She fought alongside me, and she's protected Androva too. She's one of us."

"You don't get to tell me who I can be friends with!" said Darius, his voice becoming louder. "Maybe Penny could be a magician as well!"

"That would definitely be a step too far," replied Jax, shaking his head. "Even if we knew how to do it, how do you know if we can trust her?"

"Hold on a minute," started Shannon, not liking the turn the conversation had taken.

"You were the one that made Shannon a

magician," said Darius, pointing his finger at Jax. "You know you were. If you hadn't started harvesting from the tree right next to her, her spark might never even have happened."

"We don't know that for sure," said Jax. Shannon was looking from Jax to Darius and back again as she listened to them, unable to believe what she was hearing.

"You're not being fair," added Darius heatedly, snapping a twig with a loud crack as he took a step towards Jax. "I don't even want Penny to be a magician anyway. I just want to be friends with her!"

"Keep your voice down," responded Jax. Then in an ironic moment of role reversal, he said to Darius, "There's no need to lose your temper."

"Well, you'd know all about that! Since you lose your temper more often than you change girlfriends! And we all know that's a lot!" shouted Darius.

There was silence as the echo of Darius's loud words died away.

"The portal is open," Shannon said in a small voice when she noticed the shimmer rising in front of her. Darius, unable to meet Shannon's eyes, immediately walked through it. Jax cleared his throat, not sure what to say.

"I…" he tried.

Shannon shook her head miserably. "You've

got to go," she said. Jax tried to reach out to her, but she stepped backwards out of his reach. Then, before she could change her mind, she spun round and ran along the path, knowing Jax would not have time to follow her. She had tears in her eyes before she had travelled more than a few metres.

Jax watched her go, desperately wanting to run after her, but aware that he only had a few seconds before his father would step through the portal to find out where he was. Reluctantly he turned around. Saturday, he thought. We can sort it all out on Saturday.

For Shannon, the next two days were terrible. She had received three enthusiastic texts from Penny before she had even gone to bed on Wednesday evening, which she struggled to reply to.

Then the following morning, all Penny wanted to talk about was Darius and, to a lesser extent, Jax. Shannon's other friends were also full of questions about the two boys, with even Patrick saying they were "kind of cool." It got to the point where she wished she could use a Distraction Spell to make everyone forget that they had even met Jax and Darius.

But even if she could have carried out that complicated a spell, she felt sick at the thought of using magic. What if someone saw her? The idea that she might have put Androva in danger by some of her previous actions was horrifying.

Androvans had kept everyone safe from Angelus for hundreds of years. The least they deserved was to enjoy their freedom now.

The only good thing was that Tammy really had forgotten all about Boris the Bear and any previous memory she might have had of Jax. And Shannon's mother made no mention of it either.

When Saturday morning arrived, Shannon had decided that she was going to wait for the portal as usual.

She had debated with herself whether she should go to Androva or not, and had resolved to face the situation head-on. It wasn't as if she could just stop being a magician, even if she wanted to. Which she most definitely didn't.

She looked at herself in the mirror as she tied her hair back in a French plait. Usually she wore no make-up when she went to Androva, but today she decided that she was going to put some on. Terran girls wear make-up, she said to herself, and I'm a Terran girl.

She waited apprehensively for the portal to open, half expecting it not to. When the tell-tale shimmer vibrated in the air, she took a deep breath before stepping into it. The sun had been shining brightly through the trees, so it took a couple of seconds for her eyes to adjust. Jax and

Darius were both standing there waiting for her.

Jax looked at Shannon warily, noticing her black eyeliner and lip gloss. She looked beautiful, but also defiant, as if she were challenging them.

"Shannon, I am so, so sorry," began Darius, his voice quiet. "I was angry at Jax, not at you."

"I'm sorry too," said Jax. "I said some terrible things. I never meant to suggest that Penny can't be trusted."

Shannon waited for a moment, feeling weak with relief. "Are you two friends again?" she asked cautiously.

"They are," came a deep voice from the doorway, and Revus stepped forward. "I would like to add an apology on behalf of the Council. We did not mean for you to carry this burden alone. Had we known this was how it would appear, I would have spoken to you sooner."

His eyes had a kind expression that Shannon had not seen before.

"Yes, there is a risk to all this. Terra, like all worlds, has good people and bad people. If the wrong kind of Terran finds out about Androva, we are well aware that might create problems for us. We expect the three of you to take all reasonable precautions to protect the gateway between our two worlds."

He smiled at her, and Shannon gave a tentative smile back. "But there is no point in Jax and

Darius travelling to Terra if they cannot talk to other Terrans, learn from them, and yes, form friendships with them," Revus added.

"From this first visit, Jax has acquired a new-found respect for the rules, and Darius has been brave enough to pursue a friendship against Jax's wishes. I would call that a successful outcome," he said to Shannon, who smiled without reservation this time.

"When you describe it like that..." she replied.

Jax grabbed her hand.

"Do you forgive me?" he asked. She nodded.

"And me?" added Darius, less confidently. Shannon nodded again.

"Good," said Revus. "Now Shannon, I have something to tell you later. And I have something to ask of you as well. Perhaps the three of you would join me for lunch at midday so that we can discuss it?"

Shannon agreed, and after they had climbed up to the main hallway, Revus left them alone for the rest of the morning. After a few moments of awkwardness, the three underage magicians were firm friends again.

Darius wanted to know what had happened with Penny. He half expected that Shannon would have told Penny to forget all about him after the horrible argument in the woods.

"It did cross my mind," Shannon admitted.

"But I'm not sure it would have worked anyway. For some crazy reason she really likes you," she added, with a smile to show that she was joking.

They made plans for Jax and Darius to return to Terra on the following Thursday.

Shannon mentioned that the amusement park trip was going ahead, saying that Jax and Darius would be really missing out if they didn't go. And Penny was dying to see Darius again, of course. She had agreed to cover for Shannon that Saturday as usual, but only if Shannon set something up with Darius for another time.

Shannon explained that on Tuesday she had to go to InterPharm. She would travel into the offices with her father and spend the day there.

She didn't really want to go, because her potential future career as an InterPharm employee was the last thing on her mind at the moment. But she knew she couldn't get out of it.

At lunch, Revus said the Council were extending an official invitation to allow Shannon to start attending the Seminary of Magic. Shannon's face lit up. This was like a dream coming true.

The chance to learn about all six magical disciplines, so that she could become a proper magician and fill in the gaps in her knowledge, was what she had been waiting for.

Then Revus reminded Shannon that he had

something to ask of her as well. He described the problems Androva was having with its fruit-bearing trees and plants. He asked Shannon to help them find a way to fix the problem.

"Terra is such a green world, with so much living magic," Revus explained. "And you are a very powerful magician, even if you are not properly trained yet. We are hopeful that you might be able to find a solution that we have missed."

Shannon swallowed nervously. "I'll do my best," she replied.

When she left Androva that evening, everything seemed to be back on track. She took with her some handwritten pages that the Council had prepared regarding her enrolment at the Seminary.

Revus assured her that these held a subtle Distraction Spell, and when opened, they would appear to be registration papers for a Terran summer camp. Shannon was relieved that she wouldn't have to ask Penny to lie for her any more.

As she said goodbye to Jax, Darius having gone back home earlier, she stared at him.

"You'll understand this after you've been to the amusement park," she said, "but being with you is a bit like being on a rollercoaster."

He gave her a quizzical look, and she laughed.

Then she left to go back home, already excited about Monday morning, when she would return to attend her first full day of teaching at the Seminary of Magic.

17 First Morning At The Seminary

Shannon hardly slept on Sunday night. At least half of her excitement at attending the Seminary had turned to anxiety. She kept waking up from the same horrible nightmare, where she got every single spell wrong.

All she could hear was the sound of Hesta laughing and laughing at her, before walking off arm in arm with Jax.

Eventually she gave up on trying to sleep. Even though it was early, because it was summer, the sky outside was already getting light. Shannon went down to the kitchen to get herself a glass of water, and sat outside on the patio for a few moments, letting the living magic in the garden soothe her fears a bit.

She got up to have a closer look at a couple of the more vibrant flowers, remembering what

Revus had asked her about designing some kind of Rejuvenation Spell.

She experimented with drawing out the living magic from the different types of flowers, noticing that if she really concentrated, each one felt slightly different. Sometimes the speed of vibration from the buzzing was faster or slower, and sometimes it felt heavier or lighter against her hand.

Weird, she thought. I wonder if my magic feels different from Jax's magic?

"Shannon?" came her mother's voice from inside the house. "What are you doing out there?"

Shannon nearly jumped out of her skin. Fortunately she had deliberately kept her back to the house so that no one looking at her would be able to see what she was doing.

"Mu-um!" she said reproachfully. "You scared me half to death."

"I'm sorry, Shannon, but it's nearly eight o'clock and you're standing in the garden in your pyjamas. Don't you have to be on the bus to summer camp in twenty minutes?"

"What?" shouted Shannon in disbelief. "Eight o'clock? How did it get so late?"

She ran into the house and up the stairs to her bedroom, very grateful that she would be able to use a Cleaning Spell. She would never have had time to do everything otherwise, because her long hair took ages to dry when she washed it the normal way.

Shannon had chosen her outfit the night before. She was going to wear black skinny jeans, black-and-white trainers, and a dark purple T-shirt.

She had decided that her first day at the Seminary was not the time to be wearing brightly coloured Terran clothing. She did put on a little bit of make-up though, since it helped her self-confidence and Jax seemed OK with it.

Calling goodbye to her mother, Shannon ran out of the front door, intending to go straight to the portal, as she only had a minute or two until it was due to open.

She was just checking her watch, when she nearly bumped into someone standing on the pavement outside her house. It was the new neighbour.

"In a hurry?" he asked her. "I would like to take a little of your time if I may. I was on my way to introduce myself to you and your parents, now that I've settled in a bit."

Shannon's expression went from apologetic at nearly having collided with him, to alarm as she realised who he was. He was still dressed all in black, and his face was still quite stern.

She started to back away towards the woods.

"I'm sorry, but I'm late…" she said, wishing she didn't sound so guilty. She really didn't want to get drawn into a conversation, not right now, and certainly not with someone she was secretly rather scared of.

"Someone should teach you some manners," he replied, his expression going from stern to angry. "I'll be watching you," he continued, raising his voice as Shannon started to walk away. "I don't care how late you are, you're not cutting through *my* garden again!"

Shannon shook her head and turned to run into the woods. What a horrible man, she thought. I'm sure I would still find him creepy, even without Patrick's stupid website about the kidnapper.

She checked behind her a couple of times as she ran, just to make sure he wasn't following her or anything.

When she arrived at the portal location, it was already open, so she stepped straight through it. She stood rather breathlessly on the other side for a moment until her heart rate returned to normal. Jax looked at her in surprise.

"Who are you running from?" he joked.

"What do you mean?" replied Shannon abruptly. "Does it really look like I'm running from someone?"

"No-o-o," said Jax slowly. "It was a joke."

Folding his arms, he added, "You know, a joke? You're always telling me that I can't take a joke, so I thought you were an expert on the subject!"

Shannon shook her head slightly.

"No, I mean, yes, I get that it's a joke, it's just that there was this guy…" Then she shook her head more firmly. "But I'm being silly, don't listen to me."

Before Jax could answer, she walked forwards and started climbing the winding stone staircase.

"Come on, I don't want to be late on my first day!" she called down to him.

The Seminary Board of Professors had decided that Shannon should have an identical schedule to Jax in her first week, while she was evaluated. This meant that she would also be in the same class as Darius most of the time, as the two boys were very evenly matched in ability.

Shannon hoped that she would not see very much of Hesta. If Hesta wasn't a powerful magician, then surely she wouldn't be in many of the same lessons as someone like Jax?

This was partly correct. Although underage magicians started splitting off into more specialised groups quite early on in their Seminary training, some of the classes remained common to everyone. Unfortunately for Shannon, this included classes on Mondays.

Jax explained it to her as they walked. Despite

Shannon's comment about being late, they actually had plenty of time. They had deliberately agreed on an early portal opening to make sure of it.

Jax said that for magicians of their age, Mondays were reserved for Universal Spells. These were considered achievable for every single magician, irrespective of magical ability. The whole year group spent the day in one of the large training rooms, and different professors came in for different lessons.

"Give me an example of a Universal Spell," asked Shannon anxiously. "Will I be able to do them?"

"Easily," replied Jax reassuringly. "We're only talking about things like strengthening your Solo Transference ability, or remedies for basic problems. The Manipulation part is usually the most interesting, just because there are so many options and everyone's results are different.

"Last week Cassia made the most amazing Illumination Spell. It was like a spinning firework, in all the colours of the rainbow!" He smiled as he remembered it.

"Well, it certainly beats double Maths, which is what I have on Mondays usually," said Shannon.

"Your Terran school subjects are so serious," observed Jax. "I was reading through that booklet we were given on the Open Day, and I couldn't believe it. If you didn't have your fiction books and your sports, it would be severely depressing."

"Some people like Maths," said Shannon, her expression indicating that she was not one of them.

"But what's it *for*?" asked Jax, puzzled. "Once you know how to count, and measure spells, and calculate remedies, what else is there?"

"All that technology only exists because of Maths," replied Shannon gloomily. "On Terra at least, there's no escaping it."

The Seminary was visible now, and there were several other underage magicians on the paths around them. Shannon was horrified to see that a few of them were wearing what looked like pink badges with silver letters on them. She looked at Jax incredulously.

"I thought you and Professor Alver were going to fix that?" she asked. "Don't tell me that there's still some kind of pink craze going on?"

Jax looked uncomfortable.

"I tried, but no one seems to believe me when I tell them that it was just a hoax. They think I'm just trying to prevent them from figuring it out."

"But didn't they believe Professor Alver either?" said Shannon desperately. "This is awful. I feel like we're making a fool out of loads of people. When they finally figure it out, they're going to hate us."

"Professor Alver told me that after having given it a lot of thought, he would not intervene," Jax responded. "He said that it was a good lesson for everyone about the power of a rumour. Even for him."

Shannon grimaced. "I'm so embarrassed. What must he think of me?"

"I might be wrong, but I think he finds it funny," said Jax hesitantly. "And he also said that it could lead to better student performance in his classes. I mean, because everyone knows he set me the original assignment, and they're dying to figure it out."

They had nearly arrived at the Seminary entrance.

"OK," said Shannon, taking a deep breath. "I'm not going to worry about it then. I certainly have enough else to think about today!"

There was a large registration book on an intricately carved wooden desk at the entrance. Each student signed in with their name and their Sygnus.

Shannon obviously didn't have a Sygnus, so she just signed her first and last names. She was disappointed to see Hesta's name on the page already. Sticking close to Jax, she followed him into the training room. Conversation stopped as they entered, with everyone looking curiously at their new Terran classmate.

Shannon saw Hesta whisper to the girl next to her, and then they both giggled. She gritted her teeth, determined not to let it bother her.

Jax introduced her to a few of the other underage magicians, who were all very friendly, and Shannon started to feel a bit better. Then Darius arrived, and Shannon's confidence returned almost to normal.

The first discipline was Physical, with Professor Octavian. Shannon had not met him before, but his friendly brown eyes and enthusiastic demeanour soon put her at ease.

"Come on, everyone, time to wake up!" he called, clapping his hands. "I want to build on the last lesson, so we're going to continue with our diving. And I don't want anyone banging their heads this time, so let's try not to *completely* sacrifice control for speed, shall we?"

Shannon hung back at first, watching to see what everyone else did. She soon realised that Professor Octavian wanted them to use Solo Transference to rise to the highest windowsills at either end of the training room, balance there for a few seconds, and then dive towards the floor.

He described the perfect dive as having "force *and* finesse," demonstrating himself first so that everyone could see what he meant. Shannon's eyes were wide. It looked just like diving off the highest board in a Terran swimming pool, but with no water to break your fall. The only way to control your landing was by projecting your magical force field. It took skill and practice to time it exactly right.

She found herself standing next to Darius, as Jax was one of the first to dive. He made it look easy, swooping towards the floor effortlessly. Shannon turned to Darius, about to say that she didn't think she could do it, but he stopped her.

"It's not as hard as it looks," he said reassuringly. "Wait until a few more people have dived, though. There's quite a range of abilities, and that should help your confidence."

Shannon looked sceptical. But she was soon caught up in the excitement of the activity, and her curiosity eventually overcame her fear. Her first two attempts were rather slow and uneven, while she got used to the sensation of falling. But on her third attempt she decided to trust her magical ability and go for it.

As she paused on the windowsill for a second, her toes curling over the edge, she felt the reassuring power of her force field supporting her. Then she put her arms behind her back and dived forwards.

The ground came rushing up to meet her, but she didn't stop herself until right at the last minute. She hovered for a few seconds, her heart racing, before placing her trainers carefully back onto the floor.

A few of the other students gave her a round of applause, and she stared at the ground in embarrassment. She felt a nudge against her shoulder and looked up to see Jax grinning at her.

During the break which followed, Professor Octavian set up an obstacle course running the length of the training room. Using the tables and chairs which had been stacked around the edges of the room, he created a series of walls and tunnels, and then he covered them in a green Shielding Spell.

The students would have to use Solo Transference to go over the walls and under the tunnels, without touching the floor, in the fastest time possible.

If they were unlucky enough to touch the Shielding Spell, they would receive a jolt of magical energy, similar to a Terran receiving an electric shock. This would probably cause them to fall to the floor and forfeit their turn.

You could either be careful and end up with a slower time, or be fast, but run the risk of touching the spell and falling.

There was just as much cheering and excitement as everyone took their turn as there had been during the basketball match at the Open Day.

Shannon took it slow and steady, scared of touching the Shielding Spell. Darius tried to go very fast, and almost made it to the end before his foot caught the edge of the last wall. The spell stabbed his force field, and he fell to the floor in an undignified heap with a yelp of pain.

Jax went last, his preferred position so that he would know what time to beat. And beat it he did. The combination of Jax's magical ability, his reflexes, and his utter determination to win were unstoppable. In this kind of test, no one could touch him.

Shannon was very impressed. "That was awesome!" she whispered to him, as he came back to stand next to her. The rest of the class was still cheering, and Professor Octavian congratulated Jax on another record time.

"How do you like the Seminary so far?" Jax asked Shannon with a grin.

18 Building Blocks

"It's completely amazing, *obviously*," replied Shannon with a broad smile. "I know you guys are used to magic and everything, but even you must find it kind of cool to be diving through the air."

"Racing the clock over the obstacle course is more fun," said Jax. "The diving thing is a bit boring."

Shannon laughed. "You've never sat in a double Maths lesson. *That's* boring!"

They walked off to lunch, still arguing about what was good and bad about school on their two worlds. Jax told Shannon that most Androvans would find video recordings much more amazing than Solo Transference.

While they were eating, they were joined by two of Jax and Darius's other friends, Atticus and Hadrian, plus Hesta and a girl called Sabina. Shannon watched Hesta warily, but to her relief, the other girl did not pay her any particular attention.

Smiling prettily, she asked Jax to "Please, please tell us all what the P on your secret Sygnus badge stands for? Come on, Jax, for me?" she added, putting her hand on his arm briefly. "You can whisper it to me if you don't want everyone to know. I can keep a secret."

Pass me the sick bucket, thought Shannon disgustedly.

Darius nearly laughed at the expression on Shannon's face, but quickly turned it into a cough before Hesta noticed.

"There's nothing to tell," said Jax with a sigh. "Really, there isn't."

"What about your trip to Terra then?" interrupted Hadrian. He had brown curly hair and an eager look in his light brown eyes. "What's it really like during daylight? Is it true that there are no magicians at all?"

"Only one," replied Jax. He and Shannon smiled at each other for a second, and Hesta tried to hide a scowl.

"And Terra is kind of cool. People our age have these devices which keep them connected to everything, all the time. They can send messages, play games, hear each other, see each other, and even take moving copies of the world around them."

Hadrian and Atticus looked disbelieving. Then Atticus turned to Shannon, his face curious. "Can I see one of these devices?" he asked her.

"I'm sorry, I don't bring it with me to Androva. It stops working when it goes through the portal," she apologised.

"Convenient," muttered Hesta under her breath.

"What did you say?" asked Shannon, a bit sharply.

"I said what a shame!" replied Hesta brightly.

"I'm working on an idea to solve that," said Darius. "There's someone on Terra I want to be able to send a message to." He blushed a little bit, thinking of Penny.

"Who's that then?" asked Hadrian, sensing Darius's embarrassment. "Not a *girl*?" he teased.

"I hope not," said Hesta in a slightly irritated voice. "Aren't Androvan girls good enough for you anymore?"

Sabina looked at her oddly. If she didn't know better, she would say Hesta sounded jealous, and that was impossible. Hesta was the most popular girl at the Seminary.

Darius also looked at Hesta thoughtfully, starting to understand that there might be more going on here than he had first realised.

After lunch, they returned to the training room to find Professor Alver waiting to give them a

Manipulation lesson. He gave Shannon a brief smile of recognition, then returned to his usual alert and determined expression.

"Today, we will be doing Movement Spells," he announced.

There was a groan in response from most of the underage magicians. Movement Spells were considered really dull. Shifting objects from one side of the table to the other, or lifting them up and down, was not an exciting activity.

The Universal Spells of Movement were, by definition, quite basic, but essential for everyone to master before being able to advance to the more challenging versions.

Professor Octavian had used a Movement Spell to create and dismantle his complicated obstacle course in less than a minute. But he had started by moving cups and plates across the table just like everyone else.

Professor Alver ignored the protests from his students, and he set up the tables with some everyday objects.

"Some of you are just not competent enough to progress beyond the Universal Spells yet," he reproved. "Whether you like it or not. But…" he added, then paused. "If you apply yourselves diligently, I can promise you we will end the lesson with something more interesting."

Everyone exchanged glances, wondering what

the professor meant. But despite their curiosity, they settled down quite quickly to the spells he had set.

He was a fair professor, but extremely tough when punishing bad behaviour. No one wanted to be on the receiving end of a detention from Professor Alver. He was famous for getting students to carry out activities by hand that were usually performed with magic, like scrubbing the training room floor.

Shannon found the Movement Spells very straightforward. She had already had some practice at moving objects using magic, and now that she could control the strength of her force field, it was almost ridiculously easy.

She, Jax, and Darius propped their heads on their hands, feeling increasingly bored as they repositioned and then stacked a pile of books between them.

Jax moved the topmost book down from the pile, and moving his hand in the air above the book, he opened the cover. Darius then turned the first page, and Shannon, understanding the game, did the second. Then, still using magic, they each turned a page of the book, one at a time, going faster and faster until the pages were a blur in front of them.

A few other underage magicians turned round to see what was making the increasingly loud fluttering noise.

"Alright, that will do," interrupted Professor Alver as he passed them. "You may all stop," he said to everyone, raising his voice.

The class looked at him expectantly.

"Movement Spells," began the professor, "can be used to create and to destroy. Obviously the bigger the object, the greater the amount of magic required to manipulate it. Yet also the more important control becomes. It is difficult to use a lot of magic in a very precise way."

He stepped to the front of the training room and turned to face the wall behind him. The large black stones that formed this, and every other wall in the Seminary building, were rectangular and each about one metre across.

They were not held with cement, in the way that bricks and stone on Terra were joined together. They had been meticulously carved, with magic, into exact shapes that fitted together perfectly. Then a basic Retention Spell was applied to the finished structure.

Professor Alver raised his hands, which were glowing so brightly they were almost white. "Six stones," he said decisively. "No more, no less."

Without warning, there was a flash of magical energy and a sound like an explosion. A couple of girls in the class screamed, and everyone took at least one step backwards. When the dust settled, there was a hole in the wall in front of the professor, exactly three stones wide and two stones high.

Professor Alver turned back to his students and spoke to Jax. "Rebuild it," he instructed.

All at once, Jax realised why this was happening. It was the first step in learning how to build a portal room. He took a deep breath to cover his excitement, trying to appear calm as he walked to the front of the class.

The door to the training room opened, and Professor Lenora put her head round it. She had come to investigate the noise, but after exchanging a look with Professor Alver, she appeared reassured and went away.

Jax stood next to the professor, wondering where to start.

"You don't need to reshape the stones," Alver told him.

"You will learn that another time. These stones will fit back into their original places without needing to be changed."

Jax raised his hands and surrounded the first stone with magic. He lifted it very slowly and carefully to start with, trying to line it up in the empty space. He was quite surprised at how difficult it was, and he could feel his force field vibrating with the strain. The more he looked at the stone, the more he doubted his ability.

The stone scraped from side to side, making a horrible grating noise, and looking like it would never fit. Jax broke out into a sweat, aware that everyone was watching him.

And then he realised something. It was mind over matter again. He flicked a glance at Professor Alver, and the professor gave a small smile of acknowledgment.

Jax decided to close his eyes and focus on the magical energy, trusting it to line up the stone. And, obligingly, the stone fell into place with a reassuring thud and a puff of dust.

Professor Alver waited until Jax had replaced all six stones before restoring the Retention Spell. "Well done," he said quietly, putting his hand on Jax's shoulder.

Then he dismissed the class, who immediately started to talk excitedly amongst themselves. Several people asked Jax what it had felt like to rebuild part of the Seminary wall. Everyone had been shocked to see a section of their classroom demolished.

Hesta and a couple of her friends came up to congratulate him, and Hesta said, "I bet you've never seen anything like *that* on Terra!" with a sneaky sideways glance at Shannon.

"It's not a competition!" argued Darius, and Shannon smiled at him gratefully. It was good to have Darius sticking up for her.

There was no point getting into a disagreement with Hesta about what magic could do versus what machines and technology could do. Shannon knew that, as the new girl, she would just draw attention to herself in a negative way.

With Seminary classes finished for the day, everyone removed their names from the registration book on their way out. Darius joined Shannon and Jax for part of the way home.

As he left to go back to his own house, he told Shannon good luck for her day at InterPharm, and said he would see her at the Seminary again on Wednesday.

Jax and Shannon got a drink from the kitchen in Mabre House before going to sit on the windowsill in Jax's bedroom. They still had a little while before Shannon was due to return home from "summer camp."

"I've got a special lesson with Professor Alver tomorrow on Paradox Spells," said Jax. "Apparently there are others he wants me to try."

Shannon nodded. "I'd love to learn how to do a Paradox Spell myself. You'll have to tell me about it on Wednesday." Then she pulled a face. "Let's face it, whatever you do, you're going to have a better day tomorrow than I am."

"It's just one day," said Jax reassuringly. "Then you'll be back here for the rest of the summer."

Shannon sighed and turned to look out of the

window. "There are loads of people in the fields," she said in surprise. "I never noticed that many before."

"It's this plant problem. All the leaves are still drying up like they're dying of old age or something. They're trying out new spells all the time, but no one's found the cure yet." Jax stopped for a moment, remembering the lesson before the Binding Spell.

"I wasn't paying close enough attention the last time, but we'll have a lesson on it with Professor Lenora at the end of the week. She's convinced that Living Magic holds the answer, but I'm not sure."

"Why is she convinced? What has she found out?"

"Nothing, I don't think," replied Jax. "But she says the cure must be in the Living Magic of the plants that aren't getting sick."

"You mean they have a natural resistance or something?"

Jax nodded. "But every time we try to use magic harvested from a healthy plant, the damaged plant rejects it."

"What other spells have they tried?" said Shannon.

Jax shrugged, getting bored with the conversation. He moved along the windowsill to take Shannon's hands in his. "I'm not really interested in all that just at the moment. I would much rather kiss you."

Shannon looked down self-consciously, but couldn't help smiling. "What's stopping you then?" she said.

"Nothing," replied Jax. "Nothing at all."

19 InterPharm

Shannon woke up the following morning determined to make the most of her trip to InterPharm. She was getting the chance of living her dream summer at the Seminary, after all. It wouldn't kill her to be polite to her father's boss for just one day.

She dressed in her black school skirt and a red shirt, both free from any creases thanks to a well-applied Cleaning Spell. Shannon knew she couldn't compete with Toni Maxwell, but she wanted to look a bit smarter than usual. She tied her hair back neatly with a red band.

Her father drove them both to the InterPharm offices. The building was enormous, spread over seven floors, and made out of steel and glass that dazzlingly reflected the summer sunshine.

Shannon squinted as they walked to the front entrance, wishing she had a pair of sunglasses to put on. The lady at reception gave Shannon a welcoming smile and a visitor's badge to clip to the waistband of her skirt.

They travelled up in the lift to the top floor, where Toni Maxwell's office was located. Shannon's father explained that Toni was in charge of the UK operation, while the head office was located in America.

Toni came out from behind her vast desk to shake Shannon's hand, giving her a warm smile.

She looked as stunning as she had the last time Shannon had met her. In the large corner office, tastefully decorated in shades of pink and yellow, Toni looked like a summer flower.

Her make-up was light and perfect, her hair was shiny, and the peach smell of her perfume was just strong enough without being overpowering.

Shannon's father left almost immediately, giving Shannon an encouraging smile.

"We've got a busy schedule to stick to, Shannon," said Toni. "I'm going to leave you with my very capable assistant Douglas for your tour, and then you can see some of the chemists at work in the laboratory. After that you and I will have lunch and get to know each other a bit better!" She beamed.

Shannon couldn't help but smile back at such open enthusiasm. "It sounds great," she replied honestly. "I can't wait."

"Excellent," replied Toni. Guiding Shannon forward, her hand resting lightly on Shannon's back, Toni walked out of the office and into a smaller office next door.

A young man was working studiously at his computer, but he stood up straight away on seeing Toni. He had blond hair cut very short, and rather cold grey eyes, but he smiled welcomingly enough at Shannon and shook her hand.

"Ms. Maxwell, those projections on the new line are ready," Douglas said, holding out a page with a lot of numbers printed on it. "The forecast is lower than we were expecting."

Toni frowned for a second, taking the paper and scrutinising it. "Thanks, Douglas. We'll talk about this later. Please can you take Shannon down for her tour?"

Douglas nodded. He gestured to Shannon to follow him, and Toni said she would see Shannon later, looking a bit distracted as she returned to the numbers.

Douglas and Shannon descended in the lift to the ground floor. Passing the smiling receptionist, they walked into the first office, which was laid out to display the new Decora range.

"We're about to launch our new anti-ageing cosmetics line," explained Douglas, "and the marketing team are still working on the packaging and the advertisements."

Shannon picked up a couple of the items curiously. The containers were sleek and silver, and felt cool to the touch. They gave the impression of being very expensive.

There was a mock-up of a magazine advertisement showing a photo of a beautiful woman with perfect skin, staring confidently into the camera. There was a picture of one of the silver containers underneath, and the words:

"*Decora. Our best ever range, for the best ever you.*"

Douglas reached under the table and produced a glossy carrier bag filled with samples.

"Please," he said, handing Shannon the bag. "Feel free to give them a try. Of course, you're a bit younger than our target market, but I'm sure they'll look great on you." He smiled, and Shannon noticed that his smile didn't reach his eyes. She felt a little uncomfortable.

Don't be silly, she told herself, he's probably fed up at having to spend his morning showing a teenager around. He's still being perfectly polite, after all.

She thanked him for the samples and said that everything looked great. They walked around the ground floor offices, meeting some of the people who were managing the launch. It was obviously a very big deal.

Everyone seemed really busy. Douglas made a

couple of jokes with the marketing manager, and Shannon was relieved to see that he appeared to be lightening up a bit.

They climbed to the other floors, and Douglas pointed out people responsible for selling and distribution, IT support, accounting and payroll. He explained that the InterPharm range was fairly evenly split between medicine and cosmetics.

The UK market was considered the biggest after America, and Toni had been in charge of the division for nearly a year now. Eventually they reached business development, and Shannon was able to say a quick hello to her father.

At the end of the tour, Douglas offered Shannon a drink, and they sat in the staffroom for a few moments. Shannon tried to make conversation, but found Douglas quite hard to talk to.

Then they got in the lift again and travelled to the basement, which was one floor below ground. Douglas explained that the laboratory was underground for security purposes, to make sure that every new formula that InterPharm developed was as protected as possible.

He used a special security pass to unlock the door, which was large, white, and very heavy. As they walked along the corridor, Douglas pointed out the various rooms, where individual drugs and medicines were being created. He stopped at the last door on the left and opened it.

Inside, the room was much larger than Shannon had been expecting. It stretched a long way back, and the white gloss floor, white tables, and fluorescent lighting made it look like a hospital of some kind.

There were about twenty people standing at the various tables, wearing white coats and, in some cases, safety goggles while they mixed and tested various creams and liquids.

A lot of technical equipment was also visible, with machines and computers being operated by the chemists working there.

"Of course, we have a separate manufacturing plant," said Douglas from behind Shannon as she stared at the woman nearest to her. She was adding drops of pink liquid one at a time to a larger glass bottle.

"This is where we create the original recipes. Would you like to take a closer look?"

Shannon shook her head. She was feeling a bit overwhelmed by the stark white room and lack of windows. Knowing that she was underground was also a bit creepy.

"Alright, that's not a problem," replied Douglas politely. "It's nearly time for your lunch with Ms. Maxwell anyway. Let's return to the top floor and you can wait in her office."

Shannon agreed, and left the laboratory with relief. On hearing the white security door close behind her with a heavy clunk, she was glad to be on the other side of it.

Back in Toni's office, Douglas left her alone. Shannon walked to the windows to admire the view for a few minutes. There were many pink and yellow roses on the windowsill, looking magnificent in the summer sunshine. They were very suited to Toni and her graceful beauty.

After a quick glance behind her, Shannon reached out to test their living magic. She wanted to see how it compared to the other plants she had examined back home in her garden. It all felt the same. I was right then, she thought. If the plant is the same, then so is the magic.

Then she saw that one of the pots held a rose that was looking past its best compared to the others. I wonder, she thought. I wonder if I can transfer some living magic to it and make it better. Jax said Professor Lenora already tried that, but maybe if the plant is absolutely identical...

Checking once again that no one was coming, she moved the older rose next to one with younger flowers. Carefully she drew some magic from the younger plant, until the air above it was buzzing with a visible silver shimmer.

At first when she just tried moving it above

the older rose, nothing happened. The magic dispersed and the older rose looked as sad and brown as before.

Undaunted, Shannon tried again. She tried forming the harvested magic into different shapes and densities, but success continued to elude her.

Eventually she tried applying the magic as if she were creating a Remedy, one silver droplet at a time. She held her breath as the older rose gradually came back to life. Wow, she said to herself. It's working!

She stepped back, holding her glowing hands to her cheeks, which had gone a bit red with excitement.

"Shannon, I'm so sorry for keeping you waiting..." came Toni's voice.

Shannon spun round, frantically suppressing her force field and lowering her eyes to try to prevent Toni from seeing her expression. She knew that her face would be showing a combination of delight at her discovery mixed with panic at having been interrupted.

"What's the matter?" asked Toni, with concern. "Are you OK?"

"The view..." Shannon improvised. "I think I must be a bit scared of heights, and now I feel a bit dizzy..."

Toni took Shannon by the arm and guided her to a chair. "I'm so sorry, my dear, I suppose we are quite a long way up." She poured Shannon a glass of water and waited for her to recover with a sympathetic expression.

"Are you feeling up to eating?" Toni eventually asked, and Shannon hastily reassured her that she was fine.

Toni escorted Shannon to a nearby Italian restaurant, where they had a very pleasant lunch. Toni was just as charming as she had been at the dinner with Shannon's parents, and Shannon soon relaxed.

They discussed the InterPharm student training programme, and Shannon expressed her concerns at working underground. She said that she was much more interested in the packaging design and advertising part of the business.

"A girl after my own heart!" laughed Toni. "I enjoy the selling much more than the chemistry as well. You can develop the best product in the world, but if you don't sell it properly, no one will buy it."

She suggested that Shannon sit in on the filming of the commercial that was taking place that afternoon, and Shannon agreed enthusiastically. It was really interesting to see how different uses of lighting and make-up completely changed the appearance of the model.

She left at the end of the afternoon with her father, feeling like the day had been reasonably successful.

She seemed to have got on quite well with Toni, even if Douglas had been rather more reserved, and she had enjoyed seeing how the InterPharm business operated. And of course the discovery of the harvesting transfer spell was completely amazing. She could hardly wait until tomorrow when she could explain it to Jax.

That evening, she met up with Penny, and they looked through the Decora samples together.

Penny loved the different coloured eyeshadows, and Shannon gladly let her take them. Penny's make-up tended to be like her personality, unique and a bit colourful.

Shannon preferred her make-up to be more understated, so she was going to stick with the black mascara. Though she did admit that there was a purple eyeliner in the sample bag that looked quite cool.

"You should totally wear that on Thursday," suggested Penny. "I can't believe I'm finally going to see Darius again. Are you sure he still likes me?" she demanded a bit anxiously.

"I'm certain," replied Shannon with a reassuring smile.

"What are you wearing?" Penny asked for about the twentieth time.

"Jeans," Shannon repeated. "It doesn't matter how many times you ask me, it will still be jeans."

"But what do you think I should wear?" said Penny.

Shannon groaned. "Whatever you want," she answered. "You know you won't take my advice anyway. I don't know why you always ask me."

Penny pretended to be offended. "Are you saying I *never* take your advice?" she huffed.

"Never," replied Shannon solemnly.

Penny giggled. "Well, maybe I need your advice just so that I know what I *shouldn't* wear," she said cheekily.

Shannon couldn't help laughing too. She was really glad that she had met up with Penny. It had been heavy going being around so many grown-ups all day, and she was grateful for a return to teenage normality.

Shannon wished that there had been time to try out the spell again in her own garden, but Penny didn't leave until quite late. Let's just hope I can do it again, she thought as she got ready for bed.

20 Hesta Eavesdrops

Jax was starting to think that he would have been better off going on a trip to InterPharm with Shannon. Although the summer sun was shining brightly in the sky outside, he was encased in a magical veil of ice in one of the Seminary's training rooms, and could no longer feel his arms and legs. His lips had turned blue quite a while ago, and frost was sparkling at the end of his eyelashes.

"Th-this is im-im-possible," he said through chattering teeth. "I think my magic is frozen solid. And the rest of me isn't far behind."

Professor Alver shook his head. He was leaning against the edge of a table a few feet away from where Jax was standing.

"No," he said firmly. "It is only impossible if you believe it to be so. Mind over matter."

"Th-this is like the worst Time Trial ever," replied Jax. His skin was so white that he looked like a ghost, with the only colour in his face provided by his green eyes.

"You are correct, in a way," said Professor Alver. "Time Trial is not just a test of creativity. It is also an early indicator of whether an underage magician will eventually possess the ability to do a Paradox Spell."

Time Trial was a game that all magicians learned to play at the Seminary. The object of the game was to hold a small item in the air in front of you, using magic, and keep it there for as long as possible.

Your opponents were allowed to throw any off-putting spell they liked at you, to try to reduce your time. No Combat Spells, or any spells causing physical pain, were permitted. But apart from that, anything was allowed.

However, what was happening to Jax right now was different to a Time Trial game. For a start, Professor Alver was not an underage magician, and therefore the strength of the spell he was using to restrain Jax was significant. He was also asking Jax to do a bit more than hold an object in front of him. He was asking him to do a Combat Spell.

Performing a Combat Spell against an experienced professor would be a challenge even under normal conditions. But most importantly, Professor Alver had not allowed Jax to fight back until his icy bindings were decisively in place.

Under any other circumstances, no magician would have stood obediently still while they were incapacitated in this way. This meant that Jax was in a situation he had never encountered before.

Despite his natural magical ability and his determination to do well, all he could think of was the cold. It was sapping his will to do anything.

"Jax," warned the professor, seeing that Jax was giving up. Jax closed his eyes. "Jax!" repeated Professor Alver more loudly. "This is not a game! If you don't use your magic to overcome my spell, the cold *will* cause you to lose consciousness!"

Jax opened his eyes again and gave a weak smile. "There are a f-few magicians on the Council who m-might thank you for that," he said through lips that were totally numb.

"Nevertheless," replied Professor Alver, hiding a sigh of relief, "I would rather not have to revive you." Then he had an idea, and added, "However, if I have overestimated your abilities, then of course I apologise."

Jax gritted his chattering teeth together. As the professor had hoped, that last comment had revived Jax's willpower. He closed his eyes again, but this time it was in order to concentrate, rather than to surrender.

He instructed his force field to expand, and as the silver glow became trapped in his icy limbs, he used every ounce of mental strength he possessed to drive it forwards.

He imagined that his magic was detaching from his emotions and his body, with only his mind to control it. He wanted to look down at his hands to see if it really was working, but then realised that even a second of doubt could extinguish his force field, so he ignored the impulse.

He opened his eyes, and with a shout of triumph, he sent a Containment Spell at Professor Alver. The professor was completely taken by surprise at the strength of Jax's spell. He pushed the table backwards with a loud screeching noise as he instinctively moved away to avoid the band of magic tightening inside his head.

Jax, standing straighter as his magic started to offset the effects of the cold on his body, pushed the spell forward with all his might.

Professor Alver found he could not fight the containment band and still keep Jax encased in the magical cloud of ice. As the professor's spell weakened, Jax felt the warmth returning to his body. For a second, he felt invincible.

Then he realised Professor Alver was politely waiting for him to drop his Containment Spell, rather than fighting back. Hastily, Jax released his spell. He flexed his hands as they completed defrosting.

"Very good," said the professor, nodding. "Very good indeed."

Jax smiled with relief.

"We will have another lesson next week," promised Professor Alver. "In the meantime, I want you to think about something. My teaching will require you to overcome different physical and emotional barriers using your magical ability. If you want to master this, it will eventually come at a personal cost."

Jax looked puzzled. He didn't understand exactly what the professor was getting at.

"Whose opinion do you care about the most?" asked Alver.

"Shannon's," replied Jax, without hesitation.

"Could you carry out a spell that would cause you to lose her good opinion? Lose her friendship? With no guarantee that you could fix it later?"

Jax immediately started to shake his head. "I couldn't do that," he said decisively. "I *won't* do that."

"Well," replied the professor, "we are some way from that test. There's no need to make a final decision right now."

Jax set his mouth in a line. As far as he was

concerned, he *had* made a final decision.

Outside the training room, in the corridor, Hesta smiled to herself. How fortunate that she had volunteered to collect that book for Professor Octavian. She didn't know exactly how she was going to use this information yet, but she was sure that it would prove very useful. Very useful indeed.

The following morning, as they walked to the Seminary, Shannon told Jax all about her day at InterPharm. When she described all the time, money, and effort that was being put into the launch of the new Decora line, Jax looked disbelieving.

"Is what you look like so important on Terra?" he asked.

Shannon looked equally disbelieving.

"Hello? Didn't you pick that up last week? Everyone taking selfies all the time, and those adverts before the film? And even *in* the film, the main characters were all stunning looking," she declared.

"Anyway, the Decora brand isn't just trying to sell beauty, it's youth as well," Shannon continued. "Anti-wrinkle this and anti-wrinkle that."

"Yes, but you can't stop getting older," said Jax reasonably. "Not even with a spell. Why pretend?"

Shannon laughed. "Don't ask me, I'm not exactly old enough to care. I just know that on Terra it's a really big deal. When I saw them filming the advertisement to get people to buy Decora's creams and stuff, they spent ages making sure that the model looked perfect."

She looked at Jax curiously. "Does no one ever change their appearance here? Aren't there any spells that can make you look prettier?"

It was Jax's turn to laugh.

"Well, there are spells that can alter physical appearance. But they're only temporary. Kind of like that decoration you sometimes wear on your face."

Shannon blushed, and Jax reassured her. "I like it. You look great either way though."

Then he continued. "Anything that affects you physically is a spell that has to be held in place. Like Solo Transference, or a Combat Spell. As soon as you drop your magic, the effects of the spell disappear too.

"I suppose if you wanted to look different— younger, better, whatever—then you could try to hold the spell all day long." His expression showed that he thought this would be stupid. "But you wouldn't be able to do much else," he added. "And when you went to sleep it would obviously stop automatically."

He wrinkled his nose. "Imagine if the prince in

that fairytale went to sleep next to Cinderella and woke up next to one of the ugly sisters!"

Shannon grinned at the thought. "I guess on Terra no one cares if it's temporary. And the whole point about Cinderella was her inner beauty. Or did you miss that?"

Jax grinned. "I think the prince would still find it a shock. You can't tell me he didn't notice her looks."

"No," Shannon admitted. "What about Remedies, though? They affect you physically. Are they only temporary too?"

Jax nodded. "They give your body the chance to get better on its own. I mean, if you didn't take a Portal Remedy, you wouldn't feel tired forever. But the Remedy hides the symptoms until your body catches up."

Shannon thought about this, then nodded. It was no different from taking a painkiller after all. Noticing that they were nearly at the Seminary building, she started to tell Jax excitedly about the harvesting transfer spell.

For a moment, he was shocked that she had taken such a risk by using her magic in an open office. But after she had reassured him that she hadn't been found out, he started to question her more closely about the spell itself. They resolved to try it again on Terra the following day, after the amusement park trip.

Shannon's second day at the Seminary was just as much fun as her first. She joined Jax and Darius in an advanced Combat class in the morning with Professor Livia. This particular professor had been looking forward to meeting the Terran who had famously immobilised two Council members.

The lesson was fast and furious, with the six underage magicians splitting up into two teams. The first team to completely incapacitate all members of the opposing team would win.

Professor Livia put Shannon with Cassia and Hadrian, against Jax, Darius, and Atticus. Because Jax and Darius usually won all their Combat matches when they were on the same team, the professor was curious to see what would happen when they were fighting against Shannon. She allowed them a few minutes to discuss tactics, and then they began.

Shannon began by using the Immobility Spell on Jax, which was exactly what he had expected would happen. He knew he was the strongest member of his team and that Shannon would have to fight him for her team to have any chance of winning.

The Immobility Spell was the most difficult of all three Combat Spells. Hardly any magicians could perform it absolutely, in the way that Shannon was doing. Jax was, for the moment, completely outclassed.

Darius tackled Cassia, who was the weakest member of Shannon's team, and Atticus threw a brutal Containment Spell at Hadrian. Shannon moved to stand behind Cassia, who was losing. Hadrian had evaded Atticus's Containment Spell, and was sending one of his own back.

"Now," whispered Shannon to Cassia. She dropped the Immobility Spell that she was using on Jax, and turned it on Cassia.

"What the...?" Darius said, realising that his spell wasn't working on Cassia while she was immobilised.

Jax, as soon as he was released, threw a Containment Spell at Shannon, making it as tight and fierce as possible. She winced, desperately trying to evade the band while maintaining her Immobility Spell on Cassia.

Jax nudged Darius. "Help me!" he urged, and Darius added his own Containment Spell to Jax's.

Shannon couldn't maintain the Immobility Spell now that she was under attack from two Containment Spells. But Cassia pretended that it was still working. Shannon concentrated on evading the two bands in her head. With her extensive experience of suppressing her magic on Terra, she did this fairly quickly.

Then, still standing behind Cassia where her hands couldn't be seen, she touched Cassia's shoulder. Immediately, both girls sent Containment Spells at Jax and Darius, taking them completely by surprise. With Atticus still being held by Hadrian, Shannon's team won.

Jax looked at Shannon with reluctant admiration. Professor Livia beamed. She was delighted to see such inventive tactics being used in her favourite magical discipline.

In the afternoon, after a History lesson about the creation of the Council, Shannon got the chance to create some new Remedies with Professor Jonas.

Shannon thought that the professor's rather fluffy grey hair and scruffy clothes made him look a bit like a mad scientist from Terra. She thought it was very appropriate that he spent his time teaching Remedies. They created spells to treat a variety of basic ailments, including fevers, headaches, and insomnia.

After leaving the Seminary, Darius asked if he could talk to Jax and Shannon. He wanted to check with Shannon exactly how Terra's mobile phones communicated with each other. He had an idea of how to create a kind of transmitter in the portal room that would use magical energy to replicate the electrical signal generated by mobile phone masts on Terra.

Shannon agreed that in principle it might succeed. But there was still the problem of getting her phone to work on the other side of the portal. They decided to try a more sophisticated Protection Spell next time, with three layers instead of just one.

Shannon arranged a time for her to collect Jax and Darius the following morning, and then she reluctantly went home. She didn't realise, as she left the woodland, that she was being watched.

21 Rollercoasters And Rejuvenation Spells

The sun was shining again as the three underage magicians set off to meet Penny at the station. It was a short journey to the amusement park, where they were going to meet up with Naomi, Patrick, Megan, Freddy, and Leo.

Shannon had had to take some money out of her bank account to pay for Jax and Darius, but her parents were happy to allow her to do that after the successful day at InterPharm.

Toni Maxwell had sent Shannon a text the day before, saying that she hoped Shannon had enjoyed her visit, and to let Toni know if she ever wanted a girly night in together to try out the samples. Shannon's parents had been surprised and pleased that Shannon had apparently made such a friend of Toni.

Shannon had also been extremely helpful

around the house lately, which her mother was very grateful for. She didn't know that Shannon was just using Cleaning Spells to do all the housework in a matter of minutes. But Shannon figured that the outcome was the same, and what her mother didn't know wouldn't hurt her.

Right from the start it was an amazing day. Darius was a little bit shy with Penny to begin with, but they were soon getting on just as well as they had before. She was wearing dark sunglasses and red lip gloss, and her hair was wild and curly.

Darius was a bit amazed that someone so outgoing and attractive would be interested in being friends with him. He noticed that other Terran boys were looking at Penny with interest, and his confidence grew as he realised that she preferred him to anyone else.

Jax and Shannon spent most of the day whispering to each other and laughing. They were really enjoying the freedom of being out together without having to go to lessons, and without anyone staring at Shannon because she was a Terran.

Jax was finding it much easier to suppress his magic on this second visit to Terra, and it was great being surrounded by people whose only intention was to have fun.

The first ride they went on was the log flume. Shannon wanted to start Jax and Darius off with something a bit gentler than a full-on rollercoaster, just to see how they handled it.

But her fears turned out to be groundless. Both boys were hooked from their first go. Shannon had never seen Jax look so enthusiastic about anything before. His green eyes lit up a bit more with everything that they tried.

"You're a real adrenaline junkie, aren't you?" she said to him after they had tried the tallest, fastest rollercoaster in the park. Shannon had screamed her head off, but Jax hadn't made a sound.

"I don't know what that is," replied Jax, smiling, "but I'll take your word for it."

"It means you get a kick out of all this," she tried to explain. "Almost as if you enjoy being scared."

"Maybe…" he agreed, considering. "It's not like being scared though. It's like feeling alive. As if anything is possible. You don't miss being a magician when you're on a rollercoaster. You Terrans have certainly found lots of ways to make up for losing your magical ability."

Shannon glanced behind them to check that no one else had heard Jax's words. "Why do you think I got it back?" she asked him in a low voice. "Do you think it's true what Darius said about me touching the living magic that first time?"

Jax shrugged. "You were the right age. I mean,

you were a bit older than normal, but not that much. I think there must be more to it than that though. It's not as if you're the first Terran ever to interrupt a harvest before."

"*Really?*" said Shannon, surprised.

"Of course," replied Jax, unconcerned. "I told you once before that the reason the portal has a memory is so that we can go back again and correct things if we're been seen.

"I'm sure Distraction Spells have been used lots of times too. But a Distraction Spell is not the same as the Spell of Removal. There would have been other Terran underage magicians created by now if touching living magic was all that is needed."

"What's different about me then?" Shannon wondered.

"Maybe you're just weird," Jax teased, and she rolled her eyes.

"I'm with you, aren't I?" she retorted. "So I suppose I must be!"

They all had burgers and chips for lunch, and Shannon insisted on buying Jax some candyfloss afterwards.

"I know how much you like pink," she said innocently.

Darius tasted the bright blue slushie drink that Penny had bought, pronouncing it undrinkable. The boys then tried their hand at the rifle range.

Jax picked up the technique very quickly, but he soon realised it was impossible to hit all the targets in the time allowed.

He waited for the man running the stall to look away for a second, then used an unobtrusive Movement Spell to knock down the last two remaining targets. The man looked at him suspiciously, and Jax shrugged, trying to look surprised at his success.

Shannon had recognised the faint silver glow that hung above the targets for a second after they had been knocked down.

She tried to look at Jax reprovingly, but he was so delighted when he handed her the giant purple teddy bear he had won, she couldn't help but smile back.

It was early evening when they finally returned to the station. Shannon hesitated for a moment, not sure what to say to Penny. Jax and Darius obviously had to return to the portal by a certain time, and Jax and Shannon wanted to try out the harvest transfer spell before they did so.

In the end, Jax and Darius pretended to stay at the station to get a train to London, while Penny and Shannon started to walk home together.

Shannon pretended to have a headache, and said that she would stop to buy some painkillers. Penny hardly noticed. Her head was so full of Darius that she was quite happy to be left alone to think about the day.

Shannon then doubled back to meet Jax and Darius, who were sitting outside a coffee shop at the station, curiously watching the many different types of people going in and out.

"No one looks very happy, do they?" commented Jax.

"They're all on their way home from work," replied Shannon. "You're not exactly catching them at their best."

They soon arrived back on the street where Shannon lived, and Shannon couldn't help checking the neighbour's house to see if the man was watching. There was no one there, but she felt a prickle on the back of her neck all the same.

Jax and Shannon decided to go into the woods to try out the harvest transfer spell. Although there were a lot more plants to practice on in Shannon's garden, her mother and Tammy would be home, so the risk of being seen was too great.

Darius asked if he could borrow Shannon's phone while he waited for them so that he could experiment with the Protection Spell that he had been working on.

He sat on a fallen tree trunk, concentrating on the phone in his lap while Jax and Shannon searched for some suitable plants. The huge purple teddy bear that Jax had won for Shannon sat on the tree trunk next to Darius, looking as if it were staring at Shannon's phone too.

Shannon tried to show Jax the differences in the living magic. He was amazed when he experienced it for himself. On Androva, where the living magic was much fainter, he had never noticed that there were any distinctions between different plants.

And when he had been a magic-taker visiting Terra, he had just harvested all the living magic he could reach, and everything had blended into one big ball of energy.

"Maybe it is the same on Androva," he said thoughtfully. "Maybe there has to be a match before you can transfer it."

Shannon showed him how she had allowed the harvested magic to fall one droplet at a time between plants. In a repeat of what she had done in Toni's office, she successfully rejuvenated an older plant, turning its leaves bright green and its flowers vibrant.

"This could be it!" Jax said excitedly. "We might actually have a solution!"

There was a rustle of leaves behind them, and Shannon turned round, expecting to see Darius, but there was no one there. It must have been the wind, she thought, and as if to prove her right, the branches in the tree next to her swayed in a sudden breeze.

Soon it was time for Jax and Darius to return,

and Darius showed Shannon the Protection Spell he had put in place on her phone. If you looked closely, you could see a faint blue haze around the edges of the phone's case.

"As far as I can tell, it doesn't interfere with the phone working properly," Darius said. "Can you bring it through the portal tomorrow and see what happens?"

Shannon had an idea. "Why don't we film the spell?" she said eagerly. "If there's a chance the phone might work on Androva, it would be the perfect way to show Professor Lenora!"

Jax and Darius agreed, and Shannon reminded Darius how to operate the camera, while Jax searched for another pair of suitable plants to harvest from and transfer to.

After saying goodbye to the two boys, Shannon walked slowly back home with the giant purple bear, watching the video of the spell a couple of times as she did so. She actually did have a slight headache from being out in the sun all day, so what she had told Penny earlier had not been a complete lie.

She decided to get an early night, wanting to be fully recovered when she showed Professor Lenora the new spell the following day.

She was woken early by a text from Penny.

"Can't believe Darius doesn't have a phone," she had written, with a sad face emoji.

"**He's working on it**," texted back Shannon, looking at the blue glow around her phone.

"**Text me when u get back from summer camp, I need to talk to someone about him!!!**" replied Penny, her usual good mood quickly reasserting itself.

Shannon felt glad that she could now see Jax nearly every day. She would love it if she were able to text him as well, but she was still better off than Penny.

When she walked through the portal later that morning, Jax and Darius were both waiting for her. Darius eagerly asked her to try out her phone to see if it was working. Shannon laughed at his enthusiasm.

"It's working," she confirmed, after a quick check. Previously the phone had just died when it went through the portal, so as soon as she had seen that the screen was on, she'd known it was probably OK.

She was relieved. She had had to return the phone to the shop for a reset after the last time. Being without her phone even for a couple of days had been really tough.

"There's no signal though," she added, and Darius shook his head.

"No, there won't be yet. I still have to figure that part out. But at least it's working!" he added with a grin. "You can use the camera and play games and music, can't you? That will be enough of a shock for most of our friends, when they first encounter Terran technology for real."

Later than morning, Professor Lenora listened to Jax and Shannon explaining the spell they had tried. Shannon showed her the video, and a look of astonishment broke through the professor's usual composure.

"It sounds and looks like a real possibility for a working Rejuvenation Spell," she told them, cautiously optimistic. "But there is one problem we need to resolve before we can show it to the Council."

"What's that?" asked Shannon, a bit disappointed.

"Don't be discouraged," said Professor Lenora, with a gentle smile. "There is nothing wrong with your spell. But I fear we no longer have any healthy plants on Androva to harvest from. At least not that are identical to the ones that are dying."

Shannon was silent for a moment. That was certainly a problem. Then she had an idea.

"What about finding some matching living magic on Terra? There are so many different types of plants and trees. Surely we can find one that would work in harmony with the Androvan plants?"

Professor Lenora considered this. She

wondered if it was quite correct for Androva to take living magic from Terra when the old treaty had now expired.

But Shannon had already started talking again. She could guess what the professor was worried about from her concerned expression. "Consider it an exchange for my Seminary training," Shannon suggested with a broad smile.

"Alright," agreed Professor Lenora, nodding her head. "Find me a match, and we'll show it to the Council."

22 P Is For Pretend

The next week flew by for Jax and Shannon. He and Darius came to Terra several times to help Shannon search for the right kind of living magic to heal the Androvan plants. It turned out to be more of a challenge than Shannon had realised it would be.

The Androvan living magic was so subtle compared to most of the living magic on Terra. It was like the difference between a whisper and a shout. They had to search for a long time before they found anything suitable, and even then the first few attempts did not work.

At least Darius and Penny were able to meet up on two occasions, and Darius finally got up the nerve to give Penny a kiss. Keeping his force field suppressed at the same time as dealing with the excitement of his first kiss was one of the most difficult things he had ever done. But he just managed it. Penny was happier than Shannon had ever seen her.

Shannon continued to enjoy her classes at the Seminary. She was learning so many new spells. Her Headache Remedy worked much better than the usual Terran painkillers, her obstacle course times had improved dramatically, and she could now use an Illumination Spell instead of her bedside light if she felt like it, in whatever colour she wanted.

She knew so much more about how Androvan society worked and the history of their culture. And she was gradually making friends with Cassia.

Not only did Shannon and Cassia get on very well, but Shannon was glad that she could hang out with someone other than Jax and Darius on the rare occasions when the two boys were both busy.

The only thorn in Shannon's side was Hesta. She could feel Hesta's dislike from across the room sometimes, it was that strong. And Hesta was so popular, with so many friends, that Shannon couldn't help but feel at a disadvantage.

The following Thursday evening, in an overgrown part of the woods, Jax and Shannon stumbled across a plant they had not seen before.

They quickly tested its living magic, and they were both convinced it was a perfect match for the Rejuvenation Spell. Although it was late, and the sky was getting dark, they were both excited by what they had found, and Revus agreed to allow Jax to say a bit longer.

They went back with one of the containers Professor Lenora had prepared to transport the Terran plants. The container was impregnated with a Protection Spell that would surround the plant when it was placed inside. This ensured that it would come to no harm on its journey through the portal.

Jax, being more accomplished at Manipulation Spells, did the extraction, carving the plant's roots out of the earth one at a time, with a spell that glowed slightly green in the evening light.

He and Shannon agreed to meet early the following morning, before classes began, so that they could test out the spell. After a quick hug goodbye, Jax disappeared, and the shimmer of the portal disappeared with him.

Shannon suddenly realised how dark it was. She made her way as quickly as she could out of the woods, struggling to see the path in front of her. She stopped for a moment, feeling her heart racing with anxiety. Was that her own breathing she could hear, or someone else's? She broke into a run, and was incredibly relieved when she safely reached her house.

"Shannon, is that you?" called her mother. "You're a bit late. It'll be dark soon."

"Sorry, Mum, I was just talking to Penny on the phone outside," apologised Shannon. Feeling her heart rate return to normal, she walked up to her room and closed the door firmly, checking that the window was locked as well. Don't be stupid, she told herself. You're a bit old to be scared of the dark.

The next morning, the Rejuvenation Spell went perfectly. The living magic generated by the delicate curling leaves and tiny white flowers on the Terran plant they had found was a perfect match.

Professor Lenora was absolutely over the moon, and arranged for Jax and Shannon to demonstrate it to the Council at their regular meeting the following day.

Jax and Shannon were so happy that they smiled at everyone on the way to their Manipulation Class with Professor Alver. Hesta, watching jealously, was once more determined to find a way to break them up.

She was sitting in her first lesson of the day, a rather boring History lecture, when an idea came to her. A lot of the underage magicians at the Seminary were still wondering about the pink diamond shape that Jax had worn over his Sygnus a couple of weeks ago. And because he was having a private lesson with Professor Alver once a week, the mystery had not disappeared.

The fact that Jax refused to discuss it made people all the more curious.

Hesta realised that if she didn't know for sure what it all meant, then neither did anyone else. So, slightly amazed at her own daring, and also at how easy it was, she started a rumour.

First she whispered it to Sabina, who was sitting next to her in the lesson. Hesta explained that she just couldn't keep it to herself anymore. She allowed her eyes to fill with tears as she described how difficult it had been to keep everything secret.

Then she took Hadrian and Atticus to one side as the lesson finished, and she murmured her poisonous story to them as well. After that, she sought out a group of underage magicians wearing pink badges, knowing that they would be a very receptive audience. Then she sat back and waited.

Hesta was not usually in the habit of doing anything so nasty. Her popularity at the Seminary was based on the fact that she was likeable and friendly. She just believed wholeheartedly that Jax would be happier with her than with Shannon. In her mind, all she was doing was helping him to realise that fact.

Over the course of the day, Hesta's rumour was repeated many times. In the corridors, at lunch, before, during and after lessons, until almost the whole Seminary was buzzing with it. However, no one dared to mention it to Jax, Darius, or Shannon.

Jax, his mind on that afternoon's private lesson with Professor Alver, didn't notice anything. Neither did Darius, who was completely preoccupied with thoughts of how to build a magical transmitter that would be compatible with Terran mobile phones.

But Shannon noticed. She could see groups of underage magicians whispering and glancing across at her. Everyone always averted their gaze whenever she looked at them.

Shannon was used to being something of a curiosity at the Seminary, but this was something else. She couldn't quite put her finger on what was different in people's expressions, but she could tell that something was going on.

Finally, at the end of the day, when she was saying goodbye to Cassia, she realised what it was. Cassia was looking at Shannon as if she felt sorry for her.

Shannon opened her mouth to ask Cassia about it, but before she could start speaking, Cassia backed away. She almost stumbled in her haste to leave, stammering something about needing to be home early.

Shannon turned to Darius, who was standing next to her. "*What is going on?*" she said forcefully.

Darius looked bemused. "Haven't you noticed the way everyone is looking at me?" Shannon asked him.

"No…" replied Darius, confused. "People always look at you a bit differently though, don't they? I thought you were used to it by now."

Shannon shook her head. "This isn't like that."

Darius shrugged. "I haven't noticed anything out of the ordinary. Listen, do you mind waiting for Jax on your own? I'm sure he'll be finished soon." He looked a bit apologetic. "I just really want to get home to try out another version of this phone signal I'm working on."

"No, I don't mind," replied Shannon, seeing that Darius really wanted to go. "I've got some reading to catch up on anyway."

She went into an empty nearby training room, taking a seat near the door. Unable to concentrate on her book, she turned the same two pages back and forth with a Movement Spell, over and over.

"…but that's what I heard too!" came a girl's voice from the corridor. "I can't believe she doesn't know anything about it. I suppose Terrans just don't make very good magicians after all."

Shannon turned her head in shock. She held her breath, hoping to hear more.

"Yeah, it's hardly surprising though, is it?" said

a second girl. "Hundreds of years with no magic, of course she's going to struggle. I think it's amazing of Hesta to be so nice about it."

Shannon was starting to become a bit nervous. The two girls seemed to have stopped outside the training room while they continued their conversation.

"You can't blame Jax for wanting to be with Hesta instead," said the first girl. "Apparently he feels really guilty for leading this Terran girl on." Then she laughed. "But obviously not guilty enough to tell her the truth!"

The second girl laughed as well. "Professor Alver is going to make Jax do that spell soon anyway, and then she will hate him or something. So he won't have to do it for much longer. When you know that the P stands for Pretend, it all makes sense."

Shannon had put her hand up to cover her mouth, trying not to make a sound as she listened with horror to what the two girls were saying.

"But don't you feel sorry for her?" the first girl said a bit doubtfully. "The Terran, I mean. Apparently Jax has to use a Distraction Spell every time she catches him and Hesta together. If that happened to me, I'd want to die of embarrassment…" Her voice faded a bit as she and her friend started to walk away.

"Yes, but she doesn't know, does she? That's

kind of the point of the Distraction Spell…"

Shannon stood up, her legs trembling with shock. She didn't know if she felt more upset or angry. No wonder Cassia had given her such a pitying look earlier. No wonder people had been staring at her all day.

She didn't know what to do. Forgetting all about her book, she pulled open the door and stepped into the corridor.

Suddenly she just wanted to go home. She couldn't think about this while she was still on Androva. She decided to go to Darius's house to ask him to open the portal for her. It was far too early, but she didn't care at all about the Council's timetable at that particular moment.

She was walking towards the entrance when a voice stopped her.

"Shannon!" called Jax. Shannon turned to see him appear around the corner behind her. He looked very happy. "I wasn't sure if you'd still be here. I thought you might be with Darius. I've just had the most amazing lesson…"

His pleased expression faltered slightly as Shannon began to back away from him. She was staring at him as if she had never seen him before.

"What is it?" he asked.

"You tell me," she responded in a cold voice. "Apparently I'm just the stupid Terran who doesn't know anything. Isn't Hesta the one you'd rather be with?"

"What are you *talking* about?" said Jax, completely baffled.

Shannon hesitated for a moment. Either Jax was a very good actor, or he really didn't know what she meant.

"Tell me the truth," she said. "Have you been learning a spell with Professor Alver that will make me hate you? Is that going to be your next Paradox Spell? If that's really what the P stands for," she added furiously.

"What…?" Jax started. Then his eyes widened, and a look of recognition quickly followed by dismay crossed his face. "How do you know about that spell?"

Shannon gasped. "So it *is* true!" she said, backing even further away. Her eyes filled with tears.

"No!" said Jax. "It's not true, I would never have actually done it!"

He walked quickly towards Shannon, reaching out to touch her arm. She stared down at his hand as if it were poisonous, and Jax paused, his hand remaining frozen in the air for a second.

"No need to do a Distraction Spell," said Shannon, her voice shaking with anger even as her tears started to fall. "You can be with Hesta if you want to be."

"You're crazy!" responded Jax heatedly. "This is completely stupid!"

"I told you!" shouted Shannon. "I told you that you thought I was stupid!"

She turned to run down the Seminary steps, hardly able to see through her tears. Jax watched her leave, but did not go after her.

23 Capturing Magic

Shannon ran nearly all the way to Darius's house, hoping against hope that he would agree to open the portal for her. Fortunately he was alone, and she managed to convince him that she was upset about forgetting an important appointment with her parents. She couldn't look Darius in the eye, certain that he must have known at least part of what had been going on.

When she was back in the woods, she started to cry properly. After pacing back and forth for a little while, she went to sit at the base of a large oak tree, hugging her knees to her chest while she tried to make sense of what had just happened. Her emotions were all over the place.

She felt angry with Hesta and Jax for deceiving her, annoyed with herself for being taken in, and so incredibly sad that Jax was not the person she had believed him to be. She also felt humiliated. Knowing that most of the Seminary had been either laughing at her or feeling sorry for her was horrible.

Resting her chin on her knees, she wondered what on earth she was going to do now. How could she ever go back to Androva and face everyone? And she was supposed to be presenting the Rejuvenation Spell to the Council tomorrow.

She did not want to let the Council down. But the thought of Hesta's smug face and Jax's rejection just made her start crying again. Suddenly her phone beeped with a text, interrupting her thoughts, and she jumped.

Looking around, Shannon realised it was nearly dark. She hadn't noticed the time passing, and she scrambled to her feet in a panic. The text was from Penny.

"Parents not happy with state of room," she had written. **"It's pretty bad, to be fair!!! Mega tidying job needed. Really sorry!! See you tomorrow instead?"**

At first Shannon was relieved. She had forgotten that she was supposed to be spending the evening with Penny. Shannon *really* did not want to have to discuss any of this with Penny just yet.

But then she realised that she was all alone in the darkening woods, which had started to look a little sinister. No one knew where she was, and no one was expecting her.

If something happened to me now, thought Shannon, nobody would know anything was wrong for hours and hours. Then she told herself not to be stupid. You're only feeling like this because of the argument, she reasoned. There's no need to start creating imaginary fears on top of everything else!

I just have to get home, she thought. Everything will be OK there. She began to walk on wobbly legs, first at normal speed and then faster and faster, eventually breaking into a run.

The half-light made it hard to see, and Shannon ran straight into a bramble. She fought to release her foot from the tangle of branches, nearly sobbing in her panic to get free.

As she left the woods and ran up to her house, she felt temporarily better. Then she noticed that there were no lights on inside, which meant her parents and Tammy weren't back yet.

They were visiting Mrs. Blackwood's father, and staying there for dinner. Expecting Shannon to be with Penny, they were not in a rush to get home.

OK, Shannon thought, I'll just go inside and wait for them. But to her consternation, her key was not in her pocket. It must have fallen out when she had tripped over the bramble. Trying to control her increasing alarm, she looked up at the dark and empty house as if for inspiration. When she felt a tap on her shoulder, she couldn't prevent a small scream from escaping her as she jumped and spun round to see who it was.

"Locked out?" asked her new neighbour. His expression was unreadable in the low light. "Would you like to wait with me until your parents come home?"

Shannon backed away with mounting dread. Then her phone rang, and she jumped again. Looking at the screen she saw that it was Toni Maxwell.

"H-hello?" Shannon said tentatively, keeping one nervous eye on the man in black.

"Shannon," came Toni's voice, sounding so warm and welcoming that Shannon gripped the phone tighter as if holding onto a lifeline. "I just wondered if you were free for our girls' night? I could pick you up if you are. I'm on my way home from work, and I'm in the area."

"Yes!" Shannon replied enthusiastically. "I mean yes," she repeated in a more normal voice. "That would be great. I am free."

"Wonderful, see you in five minutes," confirmed Toni, before hanging up.

Shannon looked at her neighbour. "I'm being picked up in five minutes," she said firmly. "Someone is expecting me to be right here."

He shrugged and went into his house. She

could see him watching her from a downstairs window, and wished that Toni would hurry up.

When Toni's car arrived, Shannon rushed over to it, getting into the passenger seat straight away. Toni looked across at Shannon while she fastened her seatbelt, noticing her tear-streaked face.

"Everything OK?" she asked in a concerned voice.

To Shannon's dismay, she felt the tears begin to fall again. She was just so relieved to be safe, and the whole argument with Jax had been so awful.

"You can tell me all about it later," said Toni reassuringly. "I don't live too far away, and a bit of pampering might be just what you need."

By the time they arrived at Toni's house, Shannon was feeling a bit better. Toni turned on a few side lights in her lounge, highlighting the soft colours of the furnishings and making the room look very inviting.

She offered to give Shannon a mini makeover with some of the Decora products, and Shannon found herself telling Toni that she had had a fight with her boyfriend.

"Unfortunately, it doesn't change when you get older," commiserated Toni. "Boys are nothing but trouble, and when they grow into men they don't get much better!"

She showed Shannon the results of her makeover in a hand mirror, and Shannon was pleasantly surprised. Toni had applied small amounts of make-up to enhance Shannon's features, and the result was stunning.

"You're awesome at this!" complimented Shannon, and Toni laughed.

"I wouldn't be much of a CEO if I didn't know how to use my own products," she replied.

Shannon then said that she should probably ring home to see if her parents were back yet. Toni suggested that she wait a little longer while she prepared them both a drink and a snack.

Shannon readily agreed. She was quite hungry now that her emotions were feeling more under control. She resolved to go to the Council meeting and deal with whatever happened with her head held high. She was not the one who had behaved badly, after all.

She drank the lemonade that Toni brought her, finding it a bit too sweet and sticky to be properly thirst quenching. Toni chatted about a television series that she was interested in, and as her words jumbled together, Shannon realised that she was feeling tired.

The room was quite hot and stuffy, so she excused herself to go to the bathroom and splash some cold water on her face.

As Shannon turned the tap off, she heard

Toni's mobile phone ringing. She looked at herself in the mirror over the sink, wondering why everything was suddenly feeling so fuzzy. Toni's voice became a bit louder as she walked into the hallway.

"Yes, she's here. No, not quite. It won't be long though. As soon as we get her to the laboratory I want you to start working on her. We have to figure out how to capture that magic energy somehow."

Shannon watched the colour drain from her face in the mirror. For a moment the hammering of her terrified heart pushed away the waves of tiredness that she had been feeling.

"I don't care how long it takes," Toni continued, her sweet voice turning hard. "No, not even if you have to cut it out of her."

Shannon got out her mobile, trying desperately to type out a text to her parents, but she couldn't make her fingers work properly. Her eyes were so heavy.

The bathroom door opened, and Toni was standing in front of her, still talking into her phone.

"I'm pretty sure she's figured it out now," said Toni, with a malicious smile at Shannon. "Are you feeling tired yet, sweetie?" she added, pretending to adopt a concerned tone. Shannon swayed on her feet as darkness gathered at the edge of her vision.

Eventually, she could fight it no longer, and she fell to the floor. Her last thought before losing consciousness was to realise that there must have been a drug in the unnaturally sweet lemonade that she had drunk.

Toni picked up Shannon's mobile and deleted the text she had been trying to send. She took a quick look at the message history and immediately identified Penny as Shannon's best friend.

With a satisfied smirk, Toni replaced the deleted text with one that told Shannon's parents she had decided to stay over at Penny's house for the night.

It was a few hours later when Shannon started to wake up. Since passing out, she had experienced one hideous nightmare after another, over and over. Instead of scaring herself awake at the really frightening part as she would normally have done, she kept being dragged back to relive it, unable to wake up.

When she first opened her eyes she was so relieved that the nightmare had stopped that she didn't realise what was happening for a moment. Then it all came flooding back, and with a gasp of horror, she sat up.

She had been lying on a hard table, and her shoulders ached. Turning her head from side to side to try to figure out where she was, Shannon immediately recognised the InterPharm laboratory.

Only a few of the lights were turned on, and the shapes and shadows made by the equipment in the semi-darkness looked quite menacing. The lack of windows meant that it was impossible to tell what time of day or night it was.

"Well, it looks like our Sleeping Beauty is awake," came Toni's voice. She walked towards Shannon, the heels of her shoes click-clacking on the tiled floor. Her beautiful face was twisted in a cruel grimace, and Shannon's heart sank.

Any hopes she might have had that this wasn't going to be absolutely terrible were now dashed.

"What do you want?" asked Shannon, her voice high with anxiety. "Why are you doing this?"

"I want what you have," replied Toni, matter-of-factly. "I want that magic silver glow."

"What magic silver glow?" tried Shannon, hoping to brazen it out. "I don't know—"

"Oh, don't play the innocent with me!" snapped Toni, her expression furious. "I don't have time for it!" Raising her hand, she slapped Shannon viciously across the face. Shannon cried out with the shock and sudden pain, lifting her hand to her reddening cheek.

Toni took a moment to collect herself, then

carried on. "What you did to the roses in my office. What you've been doing to plants all over the woods for the past two weeks. Yes, I've seen you," she added, when Shannon looked taken aback.

"There are two security cameras in my office, and Douglas has been following you and your *boyfriend*," she continued with a nasty smile.

Suddenly Douglas stepped forward out of the shadows, and Shannon felt her heart lurch with fear. His eyes were as cold as before, and there was no pretence at politeness this time.

So I wasn't imagining it, thought Shannon. There was someone watching me. I just guessed wrong when I assumed it was the neighbour.

"I knew there was something interesting going on the first evening I met you," said Toni. "There was a sparkle in your eyes that definitely didn't come from eye drops.

"Trust me, InterPharm makes them, and I *know* the limitations of cosmetics. Then your silly little sister started talking about fairy dust, and you got such a panicked look on your face.

"I had to get you here to observe you more closely." She laughed coldly. "I didn't think it would be so easy though. A few minutes alone and you showed me all I needed to know."

She leaned towards Shannon, her mouth set in an ugly sneer.

"Do you know how much women will pay to have their skin rejuvenated the way you did with those roses?" Toni's eyes gleamed as she imagined this. "I won't have to care about InterPharm's sales and profit. I can leave this stupid job. I can stop being nice to people I despise. I'll finally be free!"

She put her face so close to Shannon's that Shannon flinched. The smell of peaches made her stomach turn. Toni spoke again.

"And, most importantly of all, *I* will be able to look young again. You are going to show me how. If you don't, or if you try to escape, Douglas here has some special medicine for you."

Toni lifted her head to look at Douglas, who opened a box on the table, and showed Shannon a syringe filled with a pale blue liquid. He put it against Shannon's neck, and she froze, feeling the needle pricking her skin.

"This isn't like the sedative I gave you earlier. You won't wake up from this one," Toni warned. "And then you'll just be a poor dead teenage girl, who had a fight with her boyfriend, and stayed too late in the woods one night. If they find you, that is."

She folded her arms and looked at Shannon expectantly. "Let's begin."

24 After The Prologue

Jax had spent the rest of the evening feeling indignant at Shannon's wild accusations. He considered going to see Darius or even Hesta to ask their opinion, but decided that he didn't want to make a fool of himself.

Nevertheless, despite his belief that Shannon was in the wrong, he felt a sense of unease that persisted into his dreams. He kept imagining Shannon calling for his help, and being unable to reach her.

He got out of bed early and waited impatiently for the clock to show the right time to open the portal. I'll apologise, Jax thought. Even though I think she was being completely crazy, I'll apologise. Then she can't have any reason to be upset. He waited for Shannon to appear, pleased that he had decided on a solution.

When, after ten minutes, Shannon had failed to walk through the portal, Jax reluctantly closed it again. *I can't believe she's not coming!* he thought angrily. *I was going to offer her an apology, and she hasn't even shown up to hear it!*

At the Council meeting, Professor Lenora asked where Shannon was. Jax shrugged, his expression like a thundercloud, and the professor wisely remained silent. The demonstration of the Rejuvenation Spell went perfectly, and the Council approved its immediate application across the damaged cultivation fields.

Once the first few plants had been healed, their living magic could be used to heal more plants, going on and on in a ripple effect. There would be no need to take any more plants from Terra.

The Council asked Jax to pass on their thanks to Shannon, and he muttered that he would do so. "When she stops being crazy," he said to himself irritably. There was some discussion among Council members about how well Shannon was doing at the Seminary, and that her polite demeanour and creative magical ability were pleasing to see.

As Jax listened to this, he suddenly realised that Shannon would never deliberately miss a Council meeting. Perhaps something really was wrong. Hopefully it was just that her parents had changed their plans. It had happened before, after all.

While Jax was walking down the steps of the Council building, he heard someone calling him urgently. It was Darius.

"There you are!" said Darius breathlessly. "I've been looking everywhere for you!"

Darius had gone to the Repository of Records that morning to search for a book on continuous spell generation to help him with his transmitter experiment.

It was there that he had finally overheard some other underage magicians repeating the rumour that Hesta had started about herself, Jax, and Shannon. He described what he had heard to Jax, whose expression went slowly from disbelieving to enraged as he listened.

"*What?*" shouted Jax, when Darius reached the part about the Distraction Spells that Jax had apparently been carrying out on Shannon, so that he could secretly spend time with Hesta.

Jax immediately spun round and started walking furiously to where Hesta lived. Darius followed him, urging him to calm down before he did anything he would regret.

When Jax reached Hesta's house, on the other side of the city, his anger had not lessened at all.

"Did you do this?" he yelled as Hesta appeared in the doorway in response to his shout. "Did you really tell those lies?"

Hesta shrank back from Jax's fury.

"Did you?" repeated Jax.

"The bit about the spell to make Shannon hate you wasn't a lie," argued Hesta in a small voice.

"It's a lie to say that I ever intended to do it," hissed Jax. "And what about everything else? You're completely delusional!"

"I like you," Hesta said, looking at the floor. "I thought you might go out with me if Shannon wasn't hanging around anymore."

Jax made a sound of disbelief and gave Hesta a look of such contempt that she burst into tears. He turned to leave, and Darius looked at Hesta disappointedly.

"What did you expect?" he said to her.

Jax then had a very long afternoon's wait with Darius before he could even think about opening the portal again. It was a big risk to open it too frequently, and Shannon usually only went back through the portal when it was evening.

Jax was not supposed to make a solo trip to Terra. He could obviously use a Distraction Spell or even an Invisibility Spell, but the Council preferred not to take the chance in the first place.

And although Jax was worried about Shannon, he had no actual proof that she was in danger. So he didn't feel as if he could defy the Council's wishes too openly.

Finally, he and Darius decided that it was late enough to risk it. Darius agreed to close the portal behind Jax and reopen it at prearranged times later that evening and the following day. Jax was prepared to spend the whole night on Terra looking for Shannon if he had to.

And so he stepped through into the half-light of a Terran summer's evening, and found the letter from Toni. Although Jax didn't know that it was from Toni, of course.

Looking at the sky, he wondered how long it would be until nightfall. Darius had already closed the portal by the time he had finished reading the letter, so Jax couldn't have asked for his help even if he had wanted to. He decided he might as well stay where he was and wait until it was dark.

He wasn't scared of the woods at night, despite the strange noises made by the nocturnal animals and the rustling of the trees. He was so worried about Shannon that he could hardly think about anything else.

Finally he heard footsteps approaching in the darkness. Then a torch was shone straight into his eyes, and he held his hand up, blinded by the bright light.

"Jax, I presume?" came the voice of a young man.

Jax nodded.

"I need you to do something for me before we can go to Shannon. Please drink this." Still pointing the torch at Jax so that Jax could not see him clearly, Douglas placed a small bottle on the ground between them.

Jax half laughed in disbelief. "I'm not drinking that!" he said. "It could be poisonous!"

"Do you *want* to see Shannon again?" said Douglas, in a tone of voice that made it clear he thought Jax was being completely stupid. "I fear that my director is close to losing her patience. If we are late, Shannon may simply not survive the delay."

Jax swallowed. "How do I know that I can trust you?" he asked.

"You don't," replied Douglas. "But what choice do you have?"

"What is it?" Jax said suspiciously as he picked up the bottle.

"It will make you sleep," came the reply. "We don't have complete confidence that you will co-operate on the journey without some... how can I put it? Some insurance."

Jax opened the bottle and sniffed the liquid. It smelled sweet and lemony. Before he could change his mind, he swallowed it in three large gulps.

"Follow me," said Douglas. "I want to get to the car before it takes effect. I would rather not drag you unless I have to."

They followed the path out of the woods and

climbed into a dark car that was parked at the end of Shannon's street. Jax glanced at Shannon's house as they passed it, but could see nothing amiss.

"What do Shannon's parents think has happened to her?" he wondered aloud.

"My director has been texting them from Shannon's phone," said Douglas. "But there, we are running out of time too. Our preference is that we obtain what we want before anyone raises the alarm, but it is almost too late for that."

Jax looked at Douglas, surprised that he had answered the question. Then he felt a chill settle over him. He realised that there was no need for the man to be secretive if he did not expect Jax to survive to tell the tale.

They sat in the car for a few moments, as Douglas waited for Jax to lose consciousness. Jax tried to fight the effects of the sedative, but it was impossible.

He had not been given as much as Shannon, because Toni wanted him to wake up again quite quickly, but it was still more than enough to knock him out.

When Jax opened his eyes an hour later, he was in the same laboratory that Shannon had found herself in. He immediately jumped off the table onto his feet and started scanning the room. His hands glowed in readiness to defend himself.

"Calm down please," said a woman, sounding almost amused. "I'm impressed by your powers of recovery, but we don't want any accidents."

Jax turned to look in the direction of the voice. He tried to keep his face composed, but couldn't help widening his eyes slightly in alarm.

Shannon was being held by the same man that had collected Jax. She was sitting on the edge of one of the large white tables, and Douglas was standing behind her.

He had one of her arms bent up behind her back, and with his other hand, he was holding the syringe of pale blue liquid to Shannon's neck. For a second, Shannon looked at Jax with an expression of total and utter defeat. Then she closed her eyes.

After twenty-four horrifying hours in Toni's company, Shannon knew what Jax did not. Toni wanted the impossible. She wanted to be able to generate her own magical energy. She wanted eternal youth. And then she intended to use it to become the richest woman in the world.

Shannon had realised almost immediately that it could not be done. No matter how hard she tried or how many threats Toni made. And Toni could not be reasoned with. There was an obsession in her eyes that was close to insanity.

Slowly but surely, during the long and painful hours, all Shannon's hope had gradually drained away. She had tried to protect Jax from becoming involved, but Douglas knew too much about him.

Jax, feeling absolutely terrified, instinctively started walking towards Shannon to try to help her.

"That's far enough," said Toni, emerging from the shadows. Jax blinked as he took in how incredibly beautiful Toni was. She laughed. "Appearances can be deceptive, can't they? But trust me, the most exquisite exterior can hide the blackest heart.

"And," she continued, her face hardening, "the most brainless looking teenager can apparently be hiding an astonishing ability to perform magic.

"Unfortunately…" she continued slowly. "Unfortunately it is of no use to me unless I can learn how to do it myself. No, let me rephrase that. *You* are of no use to me unless you can teach me how to do it myself."

She walked forward and stood next to Shannon. "Open your eyes, my dear. I want your boyfriend to see the expression in them."

Shannon didn't respond straight away, and Douglas pressed the needle a bit further into her neck. Her eyes shot open, and the defeated look was replaced for a second with a flash of fear.

"That's better," said Toni. "Do you see this needle that Douglas is holding?" she asked Jax.

Jax nodded. "Do you know what it is?"

Jax shook his head slowly, not wanting to anger Toni by giving the wrong answer.

"It is an InterPharm drug," she explained. "It causes paralysis. Very useful when given during intricate surgery, where the patient needs to be kept completely still."

Jax nodded cautiously. He understood the meaning of paralysis, even if he didn't know exactly what surgery was. On hearing the name InterPharm, he also now realised that this must be Toni Maxwell.

"However, if too much is given, the paralysis reaches the lungs and becomes fatal. The lungs stop functioning, and you suffocate."

Toni examined her immaculately painted nails for a second, then looked up, her expression alight with malice. "I'm told it's very painful."

Jax swallowed, trying not to show how scared he was.

"If Douglas injects Shannon with the contents of that syringe, nothing can save her. Do you understand me?"

Jax nodded quickly. "But what do you want?" he asked desperately.

"What I said!" answered Toni with an explosion of anger. "Don't play games with me. I want you to teach me how to use magic."

"What do you mean, teach you?" asked Jax

frantically. "You're not a magician, are you? How can I possibly teach you to use something you don't possess?"

"We are going round in circles!" shouted Toni, losing her temper. "If being a magician comes first, then make me into a magician!"

"What?" responded Jax in disbelief. "I can't *make* you into a magician. You're too *old* for that!"

For a moment there was complete silence. Then Toni screamed with rage, and Shannon knew that there was no way back.

25 An Ending

Jax stared at Toni in shock. He considered trying to use a spell to incapacitate her while she was distracted, but soon discounted that after a glance at Douglas, who was still holding the needle to Shannon's neck.

The silence that fell after Toni's scream died away was deafening. Even Douglas showed no desire to break it. Toni stood with her hands clenched into fists by her sides, her face distorted with fury. Gradually she got herself under control again, and her breathing returned to normal.

"Very well!" she spat. "Have it your way. But if I don't get to capture your magic, then neither does anyone else. You can take the secret with you to your graves."

She walked behind Douglas and took another syringe out of the box. Douglas cleared his throat, and Toni spun round to glare at him.

"What? Not losing your nerve, are you?" she

snapped.

"No." He shook his head decisively. "Never. But I wonder if it is necessary to proceed like this. It is a *very* painful way to die."

Toni considered for a moment, as if she knew what Douglas were asking. "Alright. I suppose I could be persuaded. It will be easier to administer if they are unconscious. And they will still know that death is coming for them. That will be pain enough."

Jax and Shannon stared at each other, not understanding Toni's meaning. They each wanted to give the other some reassurance, but were both aware that there was nothing they could say.

Jax was frozen with indecision, trying to decide how they could possibly escape. Shannon shook her head slightly, feeling the needle scrape against the skin of her neck. She had given up.

Toni walked to another table and picked up two small glass bottles from a larger rack. She handed one to Shannon and the other to Jax.

Douglas released Shannon's arm from behind her back, but did not lower the needle. Jax realised that the bottle was the same as the one that Douglas had given him earlier.

"Drink!" said Toni forcefully, when Jax and Shannon remained motionless.

Then Toni ripped the top off the syringe she was holding and dug it into Jax's neck. He flinched as it pierced the outer layer of his skin.

"*Drink it!*" Toni repeated, her thumb on the end of the syringe as if to start injecting its contents.

"Don't!" said Shannon, her voice breaking slightly. "Please don't. I'll drink it." With trembling fingers, she unscrewed the top of the bottle.

Douglas grabbed her hair roughly and pulled it backwards so that her neck was more exposed. She gave a brief cry of pain. He made as if to inject her, and Jax immediately began to unscrew the lid on his own bottle.

"Amazing what a little motivation can do," said Toni spitefully.

Reluctantly Jax and Shannon drank the sweet lemon liquid. Tears fell from Shannon's eyes, and Jax half lifted his hand as if to reach out to wipe them away.

Toni and Douglas waited for a few minutes, until they could see that the sedatives were starting to take effect. Then they lowered their syringes, intending to wait until Jax and Shannon were completely asleep before killing them.

"Let's go up to my office and collect the rest of the equipment," said Toni after a pause. "These two aren't going anywhere, and I want to track down the other boy before morning."

Jax's eyes, which had started to glaze over

from the effects of the drug, suddenly became alert again. Toni glanced at him and raised her eyebrows.

"Darius is his name, isn't it?" she asked Douglas, who agreed. "And who knows where Darius can lead us, and what we'll find when we follow him?" added Toni. "Oh dear, you seem worried, Jax. Never mind, in a little while you won't be worried about anything ever again."

She and Douglas left the laboratory, locking the door behind them. Jax immediately went to Shannon, who was half unconscious on the table.

"Shannon!" he said urgently. She looked at him with a faraway expression.

"I'm sorry I shouted at you," she murmured. "So sorry…"

She closed her eyes, and even with Jax shaking her, she didn't open them again. He tried to lift her into his arms, thinking that maybe he could escape while carrying her, but the room tilted around him as the sedative began to overpower his senses.

Jax leaned against the table that Shannon was lying on, letting the exhaustion wash over him. He brushed her hair away from her face with his hand.

"I don't know if you can hear me," he said, "but I'm sorry too. It wasn't your fault, it was mine…"

He couldn't hold his head up any longer. The letters on the box next to him swam in and out of focus. The long, incomprehensible name of the drug inside began with a large capital P in blue.

Suddenly, although Jax was very nearly completely asleep, his mind recognised something.

P is for Paradox Spell, his mind said. And Jax's magical force field woke up. Slightly unsteadily, he pushed himself upwards. He knew immediately what he was going to do.

This drink they had been forced to take seemed to work a lot like a Binding Spell. Concentrating with every ounce of strength he possessed, Jax created a Portal Remedy and allowed the magical droplets to fall one at a time onto Shannon's lips.

For a minute or two, nothing happened, and he forced himself to stay calm. The effort required to counteract the sedative was enormous, and he didn't know how much longer he could keep it up.

Then he saw that Shannon's mouth had opened, and she was swallowing. Desperately, he tried to keep the spell going, but eventually he was overpowered. Staggering slightly, he collapsed onto the floor.

Shannon, hearing the noise as Jax fell, woke up

properly. She licked her lips, not sure for a moment what was happening. Then she sat up and saw Jax. She immediately jumped off the table and crouched down next to him.

"Portal Remedy…" he managed to whisper, his eyes beginning to close.

Shannon realised what the taste on her lips had been. Straight away, she projected her force field, filled it with the Remedy, and let it fall from her fingertips into Jax's mouth. Within a few moments, he was awake again. They hugged each other tightly, so relieved at first that they couldn't speak.

Then Jax broke away.

"We have to get out of here!" he said anxiously. Shannon nodded. They scrambled to their feet and ran across the shadowy laboratory to the door.

It was locked, but the lock was only a simple one, and Jax used a quick Manipulation Spell to turn the bolt inside it.

They broke into a run again when they were in the corridor, stopping when they reached the heavy white security door at the end. Unbelievably, it was open.

"They obviously never expected us to get this far," whispered Shannon in surprise.

Before Jax and Shannon could go any further, the lift door pinged, and Toni and Douglas appeared. The look of shock on their faces was so absolute that it was almost comical.

Jax immediately moved between Shannon and the two new arrivals. He was feeling such anger that his body was vibrating with it.

"I have something for you," he said to Toni. Then he projected a Manipulation Spell with such force that he had to take a step backwards.

It dried out Toni's skin like the blast from a furnace. She could feel herself shrivelling up like a raisin, and looked down in horror as her hands turned into withered claws.

Jax had guessed that the most effective spell he could do would be one that made Toni look older. After her scream of rage when Jax had told her she was too old to become a magician, he realised that it was obviously a very sore point with her.

She wouldn't know that the spell would only last as long as Jax held it in place, and hopefully she wouldn't get the chance to find out.

Toni, catching sight of herself in the mirrored surface of the lift doors, which had closed, gave a wail of misery. Douglas stepped forward aggressively towards Jax, and Shannon shook her head.

"Oh no you don't," she told him. Gathering her force field in all its considerable strength, she decided to try an Immobility Spell. It was one of her best spells, after all, and perhaps she could apply it to a physical body in the same way that she applied it to a magical force field.

It turned out that she could, and Douglas froze like a robot that had had its batteries suddenly removed.

"Now what?" Shannon said, turning to Jax. Her eyes had recovered their sparkle. He grinned back at her.

"Have I ever told you that you're my favourite person in the whole world?" he replied, looking at Douglas and laughing.

"Not lately," replied Shannon, looking slightly downcast.

"Well, you are. Hesta is living in a fantasy land, and I'm sorry that you were caught up in it."

"OK," Shannon said happily. "Apology accepted."

"What shall we do with these two *lovely* people?" asked Jax, turning back to Toni and Douglas. Jax and Shannon advanced towards them, until they were close enough to see the fear in their former captors' eyes.

"Please…" begged Toni, "please don't leave me like this, I'll do anything!"

Suddenly the door to the emergency stairway burst open and four policemen rushed through it. They were followed by Shannon's neighbour, still dressed in black, and obviously in charge of the other men.

With extraordinary presence of mind, Shannon dropped her spell and fell to the floor, pulling Jax down alongside her.

"Please help us!" she called weakly. "We were kidnapped! They drugged us with something, we can hardly move…"

Jax, immediately realising what Shannon was doing, held his head as if he were in pain. Shannon caught a glimpse of his green eyes shining with mischief before he lowered his eyelids.

It took Toni and Douglas a couple of seconds to recover, but once they realised that the spells had ended, they lifted their heads angrily and started to protest.

"You don't understand, these children are dangerous magicians!" said Toni loudly. "They were holding us captive just a few seconds ago!"

"What are you talking about?" said Jax, adopting a puzzled tone. At the same time he reached up to place his glowing hand against the back of Toni's ankle.

She glanced down for a second, with a bewildered look. "I… I'm not sure," she said hesitantly. "I… was it something about roses?"

Unobtrusively, Jax patted her ankle again. Shannon spoke.

"They thought we had access to some kind of

secret formula, but that's completely crazy. We're only kids."

Douglas interrupted. "Officer, these children are indeed dangerous. I must insist that you let us explain."

"Explain what?" said Shannon angrily. "How you kidnapped us and threatened to kill us? All the evidence is in that laboratory in there," she added, pointing.

"I saw it!" shouted Douglas. "I saw…"

His brow furrowed at the same time as Jax's hand brushed against his foot.

There was silence in the room as Douglas struggled to find the words to continue.

Shannon's neighbour finally spoke. "Ms. Maxwell and Mr. Connor, I am arresting you on suspicion of kidnapping with intent to cause bodily harm.

"You do not have to say anything, but it may damage your defence if you do not mention when questioned something you later rely on in court. Anything you do say may be given in evidence."

The policemen had put handcuffs on Toni and Douglas before Shannon's neighbour had finished speaking. Suddenly they both realised what was happening and began to struggle.

"This is your fault!" Douglas shouted at Toni. "It was all your idea to kidnap them!"

"You went along with it!" yelled Toni. "They had access to our competitor's secret formula! With that we could have…" Suddenly she realised that she was incriminating herself by what she was saying, and she trailed off.

"Secret formula?" Jax mouthed at Shannon, struggling to suppress a grin.

They were both aware that a new idea introduced during a Distraction Spell was often adopted as the truth by the recipient of the spell. On this occasion it seemed to have worked incredibly well.

Still struggling, Toni and Douglas were taken away. Shannon's neighbour approached her and Jax as they cautiously stood up. Shannon pretended to be a bit wobbly from the sedative.

"Detective Inspector Marshall," he offered, extending his hand.

"Shannon Blackwood," she replied as she shook his hand.

"My local neighbourhood trespasser," he replied with a faint smile. "I know who you are. I'm sorry it took me so long to find you. Ms. Maxwell's car registration was false, and it wasn't until her accomplice turned up to collect your friend earlier tonight that we were able to trace them to this building."

Then he turned to Jax. "You're a bit of an enigma though," he added.

"I'm Jax… um, just Jax," said Jax awkwardly, completely forgetting the surname that he and Shannon had made up for him when he attended the Open Day.

"Well, Just Jax," said DI Marshall, "I think the sooner we return this young lady to her worried parents, the better."

He turned to climb the stairs, and Jax and Shannon followed him. They noticed additional policemen arriving to secure the scene and collect evidence.

"I'll have to bring you in for questioning tomorrow," DI Marshall said as they climbed into his car. "But get a good night's sleep first. I think you've earned it. If this pair of criminals are who we think they are, this isn't the first time they've done this.

"They've never actually kidnapped children before, but they've certainly broken the law to obtain information on InterPharm's competitors. There was a burglary, and the use of a fatal neurotoxin was threatened."

Shannon looked at Jax in surprise. Toni must have been truly desperate to preserve her youth and beauty, no matter what the cost. She shivered. "I guess we had a lucky escape," she said. Jax squeezed her hand.

By the time they arrived back at Shannon's house, both underage magicians could hardly keep their eyes open. Shannon's parents hugged her as if they would never let her go. They thanked Jax for looking after her, and he protested, saying that he and Shannon had looked after each other.

Shannon's mobile was still at the crime scene, so she called Penny on the landline to reassure her that everything was OK. Jax said that he must have dropped his phone in the woods when Douglas drugged him.

He explained that he lived with his father, but that he had been staying with friends and wasn't expected back until the morning. Seeing that he was nearly falling asleep where he stood, Shannon's parents suggested that he sleep on their sofa for one night.

Tomorrow is going to be interesting, thought Jax as he closed his eyes.

26 Two Weeks Later

Shannon felt the mobile phone in her jeans pocket buzz with a text. It was late evening, and she was standing at her bedroom window looking down at the shadowy woods.

"**What are you doing?**" it said.

"**Wondering about something**," she replied.

"**About what?**" came the response.

"**I'm wondering what it will feel like to use my own portal room tomorrow morning...**"

"**You'd better not be late!!!**" Jax replied.

Shannon thought for a moment before she typed her answer. It had been over a week since she and Jax had been texting each other, and the novelty had definitely not worn off yet.

Although they were together nearly every day, they still texted back and forth all the time. They were closer than ever after what had happened. Shannon had started to keep her phone on silent because she knew that the constant beeping was driving her parents up the wall.

So much had changed since that horrific night at the InterPharm laboratory. Very early on the morning after their escape from Toni and Douglas, DI Marshall had arrived on the doorstep with another police officer to get Shannon and Jax's side of the story.

He suggested that he question them at his house rather than at the police station so that it wouldn't be so intimidating for them.

"Although," he added thoughtfully, "something tells me that the two of you are not easily intimidated."

DI Marshall had arrived before Jax had time to go back through the portal to reassure Darius, and Jax was starting to feel a bit uneasy about the delay. But he didn't see how he could walk off with DI Marshall standing there, waiting expectantly for Jax and Shannon to finish their breakfast.

Shannon offered to give her version first. She had been thinking a bit more about what to say, particularly about the secret formula idea she had come up with the night before.

She wanted Jax to have the benefit of hearing what she said so that all he would have to do was go along with it. Shannon knew that Jax still hadn't learned enough about Terra to be able to fool someone like DI Marshall.

At first it went according to plan. Shannon's account was carefully typed into the laptop of the policeman who had accompanied DI Marshall. Most of what she said was entirely true, and she didn't have to lie about how terrifying it had been.

Jax looked at Shannon wretchedly when he heard exactly what Toni and Douglas had put her through. He blamed himself, knowing that none of it would have happened if he and Shannon hadn't argued about the stupid rumour Hesta had started.

DI Marshall stopped Shannon when he saw Jax's face.

"Don't think, even for a moment, that this is your fault," he said firmly. "Toni Maxwell would have found a way to do this eventually. She would have created another opportunity. She was obsessed."

Shannon completed her story, explaining that she and Jax had tried not to drink all of the sedatives that Toni had given them.

"I think that's why we managed to wake up a bit sooner than they were expecting us to," she added, feeling slightly awkward at the lie.

Then it was Jax's turn. He ran into a problem almost straight away when he couldn't convincingly provide either a surname or an address.

He was annoyed with himself for not agreeing on these details with Shannon in advance. They had just had no time. Shannon tried to help Jax, but DI Marshall told her tersely that she was not permitted to speak on Jax's behalf.

When Jax began to tell his story, things improved. He had, after all, not used any magic when he was captured, so all the details of his story about the needles and the threats were very believable.

And when Jax said that Toni wanted something that he just couldn't give her, this also had the ring of truth.

DI Marshall asked how Douglas knew where to find Jax, and what he had been doing alone in the woods at that time in the first place. Jax said that he had gone there to think, after the argument. Then DI Marshall asked again what Jax's real name and address were.

And then, in the pause that followed while Jax tried to think of an answer, DI Marshall pointed at the Sygnus on Jax's shoulder and asked what it was.

There was a moment of silence that seemed to last for a very long time. Shannon couldn't believe that she hadn't noticed the uncovered Sygnus earlier. Glowing silver with magical energy, it looked like a special effect that belonged more on a film set than in real life.

Jax considered what to say. He didn't want to keep lying, but equally he didn't want to expose Androva to scrutiny from Terra's police force. He opened his mouth, but before he could start speaking, DI Marshall held up his hand.

"Wait a moment," he said. Then he turned to the other policeman and asked him to go back to the station. He added that they would finish the session later, as Jax and Shannon were obviously still very tired. The man left without protest.

DI Marshall turned back to Jax and Shannon.

"Look," he began, rubbing his eyes tiredly. He had not slept the previous night. Toni and Douglas's questioning had lasted until the early hours, and they were at that moment in court, being charged with their crimes. They would be remanded in custody until a trial date had been set.

"I like you," said the DI. "I know we didn't get off to the best start," he added, with a frown at Shannon, who stammered an apology. "But I like you both. You displayed extraordinary courage and maturity in a situation that most adults would have found insurmountable.

"However, you are lying to me. Not about everything," he said, holding his hand up again to still Shannon's protest. "But there is something not right here."

Jax and Shannon looked at each other. What

could they do? Jax moved his chair to face Shannon's and took her hands in his. DI Marshall watched them slightly warily. He could feel something like static electricity against the skin on his face and hands.

Then, to his complete and utter astonishment, he saw a kind of glowing force field radiate from the two teenagers in front of him. It extended only a centimetre or so, but it was bright and buzzing with energy. As DI Marshall stared at them, Jax raised his eyebrows and Shannon nodded.

She turned towards the detective. Raising her hands, she allowed a silver glow to project from them, and the DI instinctively shrank backwards in his chair as it approached.

"Don't be afraid," said Shannon softly, stopping the glow before it reached him. "This is magical energy, in its purest form. I have not filled it with any spell that could hurt you or distract you."

"We could make you forget that this meeting ever happened," added Jax, "but we both agree that it is time to trust someone."

The DI found that his curiosity was stronger than his fear, and he reached out to touch the glow that Shannon was projecting. As his hand brushed against it, he could feel it vibrating against his skin.

"She knew," he said suddenly, comprehension dawning on his face. "Toni Maxwell, she knew about this!"

"She did," acknowledged Jax. "But she has forgotten it now," he added, his face turning hard.

DI Marshall struggled to get his head around what was happening.

"I don't understand what is going on here," he said. "I have not slept since yesterday, and I feel as if my mind is playing tricks on me."

Shannon smiled. "I felt a bit like that myself the first time," she replied. Then she went on hopefully. "Can we trust you? Will you listen before you jump to any conclusions?"

DI Marshall considered for a moment. He was a fair man, and he had been telling the truth when he said that he liked Jax and Shannon. They were brave and resourceful. And the honesty in their faces at that moment was undeniable.

He decided to suspend his disbelief before making any judgement. He nodded. And so they told him their story.

Later that morning, Jax and Shannon took DI Marshall through the portal. On the other side they first encountered a very worried Darius and then behind him a rather startled Revus. Hurriedly Jax started to explain what was going on, but Revus insisted that they take their unexpected guest somewhere more comfortable first.

DI Marshall laughed to himself as he climbed the stairs from the portal room behind Jax and Shannon.

"What is it?" asked Shannon curiously, turning back to look at him.

"I feel like I'm thirteen years old again, and I've somehow managed to bring my favourite book to life," he said incredulously. "Half of me says this can't possibly be real, but the other half doesn't care!"

When they had sat down, Shannon immediately fetched DI Marshall a Portal Remedy. He drank it without question, figuring it was a bit late to start being suspicious.

As it turned out, DI Marshall, or David, as he asked to be called, got on very well with Revus. They were quite similar in terms of their outlook on life, and soon developed a mutual respect and understanding.

There were so many questions to be answered on both sides that David ended up staying for most of the day. Jax and Shannon were relieved that everything was going so well. David agreed to protect their secret while he and Revus worked through the ramifications of revealing Androva's existence to the Terran authorities in the future. Neither man believed that it was something that could be done without a lot more information being exchanged first.

The following day, Monday, Shannon's parents were very surprised when she told them that she still wanted to go to summer camp. DI Marshall reassured them that a quick return to normality was probably the best thing for Shannon.

She was grateful for his support, realising that he might turn out to be an important ally now that he knew the truth.

At the Seminary, before lessons began, Revus gathered all the professors and students together in the largest training room. As a senior Council member, his authority extended to every part of Androvan life, and for once, on this occasion, Jax was grateful for it.

"I have called you all here to explain something. This is the word of the Council, and as such, is beyond contestation.

"The Terran underage magician known as Shannon is here with our full support, and her magical ability means that she can hold her own with any of you. *Any* of you," he repeated, to ensure that his meaning was clear. "You will treat her with respect and kindness."

Then he looked up and down his audience as if he were searching for someone in particular. Jax, who had deliberately stood just behind Hesta in readiness for this, gave her a shove forwards.

He was not very gentle, and she nearly fell to her knees. As she turned angrily to see who had done it, she saw Jax, and her face immediately filled with dismay.

"I'm *so* sorry," said Jax insincerely, his green eyes cold. "But I think my father is looking for you."

Hesta looked back at Revus apprehensively, and he beckoned her forward. Hesta was forced to apologise to Shannon in front of the entire Seminary, professors and students alike.

Scarlet in the face, her voice stammering, she had never felt more humiliated in her life. Shannon almost felt sorry for her. Almost, but not quite.

Later that week, Darius had a breakthrough with his Transmitting Spell. He had successfully created a replica of the Terran electrical signal that was used by mobile phone masts, and it could be broadcast by any spellstation.

Spellstations were the devices used in portal rooms to generate the shimmering doorways, so they were able to form a bridge across two locations, even different worlds, with magical energy.

Darius had intended the Transmitting Spell to be continuous, but because it used up a lot of magic, it needed to be topped up every few days.

"Kind of like charging a mobile phone," said

Shannon when Darius explained it to her.

"Exactly," replied Darius. "In fact, I think I can use a similar spell to actually charge the mobile phones when we get them. It's not like there are any plug sockets on Androva after all."

David Marshall agreed to provide Jax and Darius with mobile phones. He was taking the responsibility of protecting Androva very seriously, and he wanted to support the boys.

They would be able to integrate into Terran life much more easily on their now regular visits if they had mobile phones like everyone else.

Penny was ecstatic at being able to finally exchange texts with Darius. It was so much easier for them to build their friendship when they could stay in touch every day.

Penny didn't know anything about Androva yet, but Shannon knew that they would probably have to tell her soon.

Although Penny showed no signs of becoming a magician herself, she wasn't stupid, and Shannon didn't want to have to lie to her indefinitely. There was still no way to know why Shannon herself had first become a magician all those weeks ago. It was something that she and Jax were still trying to figure out.

Occasionally, David Marshall woke up in the middle of the night, wondering if he was imagining the whole thing. But he would only have to walk into his garage and look at the first few steps down to the portal room that Jax was building to be reassured that he wasn't going mad after all.

Professor Alver had accelerated Jax's training with the blessing of Revus. An open portal in the woods was not safe for either world, and more than that, Revus now trusted his son to use the new portal room responsibly.

David had suggested that the portal room be built under his garage so that it would be easier for Revus to visit him undetected and so that Shannon could come and go without attracting attention from her parents.

And now the portal room was ready. There were still two weeks left of the Terran school summer holidays, and Shannon intended to make the most of them.

David had suggested that he invent an exchange programme for the benefit of her parents when school restarted, to allow her and Jax to split their time between the Seminary and Shannon's Terran school. Everything seemed to be working out perfectly.

"**Late??**" typed Shannon in reply to Jax's text. "**No way!! It's Combat tomorrow and I've got an Immobility Spell here with your name on it!!!**"

Then she put the phone back in her pocket

and smiled.

The Legacy of Androva Series Continues...

How far would you go to find an explanation if you were *still* the only magician in the entire world and no one knew why?

You could try reading some ancient history books. That's pretty harmless, at least to start off with. Or you could experiment with some brand-new spells. That's a bit more risky, but still nothing you can't handle.

Or maybe you could go back in time two thousand years to question the one magician who might have the answer. That's dangerous by anyone's standards. You might get stuck there. You might die there. Or you might discover that you never become a magician at all...

Jax and Shannon return in another exciting adventure, where nothing is as it seems, and the past could be rewritten in a heartbeat.

You can find out more about the author, and the rest of the books in the Legacy of Androva series, at
www.alexcvick.com

35188022R00167

Made in the USA
Columbia, SC
20 November 2018